*"How many times do I have to tell you, she's not my daughter?"*

Tara's back straightened. "Don't worry, Dr. Landers, I already have custody of my niece and I plan to raise her like my own." Her glare was heated with anger. "But it was my sister's last request that you be told about your daughter."

Matt glanced down at Tara's ringless hand. Was she alone? He shook away the feelings of sympathy. She wasn't his problem.

"For one last time, I never met your sister."

Just then the baby stirred and began to cry. He wanted to soothe the infant…and her beautiful aunt, to take them in his arms and protect them from the world. None of this was their fault—or his!

He could not allow this little angel and her loving guardian to play with his feelings. And he would not be taken advantage of. But could he help them find the real father?

Whose child *was* Erin Landers…?

Dear Reader,

During the warm days of July, what better way to kick back and enjoy the best of summer reading than with six stellar stories from Special Edition as we continue to celebrate Silhouette's 20th Anniversary all year long!

With *The Pint-Sized Secret*, Sherryl Woods continues to delight her readers with another winning installment of her popular miniseries AND BABY MAKES THREE: THE DELACOURTS OF TEXAS. Reader favorite Lindsay McKenna starts her new miniseries, MORGAN'S MERCENARIES: MAVERICK HEARTS, with *Man of Passion,* her fiftieth book. A stolen identity leads to true love in Patricia Thayer's compelling *Whose Baby Is This?* And a marriage of convenience proves to be anything but in rising star Allison Leigh's *Married to a Stranger* in her MEN OF THE DOUBLE-C RANCH miniseries. Rounding off the month is celebrated author Pat Warren's *Doctor and the Debutante,* where the healthy dose of romance is just what the physician ordered, while for the heroine in Beth Henderson's *Maternal Instincts*, a baby-sitting assignment turns into a practice run for motherhood—and marriage.

Hope you enjoy this book and the other unforgettable stories Special Edition is happy to bring you this month!

All the best,

Karen Taylor Richman,
Senior Editor

Please address questions and book requests to:
Silhouette Reader Service
U.S.: 3010 Walden Ave., P.O. Box 1325, Buffalo, NY 14269
Canadian: P.O. Box 609, Fort Erie, Ont. L2A 5X3

# PATRICIA THAYER

## WHOSE BABY IS THIS?

Published by Silhouette Books

**America's Publisher of Contemporary Romance**

To Jennifer Nauss, for all your hard work
helping me find just the right story for Dr. Matt. It's nice
to have someone in your corner. And always, Steve.

 SILHOUETTE BOOKS

ISBN 0-373-24335-9

WHOSE BABY IS THIS?

Copyright © 2000 by Patricia Wright

This edition published by arrangement with Harlequin Books S.A.

Visit Silhouette at www.eHarlequin.com

**Printed in U.S.A.**

## *PATRICIA THAYER*

has been writing for fourteen years and has published over ten books with Silhouette. Her books have been nominated for the National Readers' Choice Award, Virginia Romance Writers of America's Holt Medallion, and a prestigious RITA Award. In 1997, *Nothing Short of a Miracle* won the *Romantic Times Magazine* Reviewers' Choice Award for Best Special Edition.

Thanks to the understanding men in her life—her husband of twenty-eight years, Steve, and her three sons—Pat has been able to fulfill her dream of writing romance. Another dream is to own a cabin in Colorado, where she can spend her days writing and her evenings with her favorite hero, Steve. She loves to hear from readers. You can write her at P.O. Box 6251, Anaheim, CA 92816-0251.

# IT'S OUR 20<sup>th</sup> ANNIVERSARY!
## We'll be celebrating all year,
## Continuing with these fabulous titles,
## On sale in July 2000.

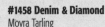

## Chapter One

Did the man deserve to know he was a father?

Tara McNeal wasn't so sure as she stood at the office door of Dr. Matthew Landers, pediatric cardiothoracic surgeon.

Had she done the right thing coming to Santa Cruz? Tara looked down at her tiny three-month-old niece, Erin Marie, strapped in the carrier against her chest. From the moment the precious little girl had been born, Tara had wanted nothing more than to shower her with everything, especially love.

But Tara had made her deceased sister, Briana, a promise. That meant Erin's father, Matthew Landers, had to be told about his daughter. Tara doubted the man cared. Not when he'd walked out of Bri's life long before he knew she'd gotten pregnant.

So why would Dr. Landers care now? But it still

frightened Tara to think he might take Erin away from her, might want to raise his daughter.

*Well, I'm not going to get any answers until I talk to the man,* she thought.

Tara's hand shook as she opened the door. Inside, the surgeon's waiting room had been decorated in soft blue and gray. A comfortable-looking sofa and four barrel chairs were grouped at a coffee table with several books scattered along the top.

At the desk sat a receptionist, a woman in her forties with dark hair and half-glasses perched on her narrow nose. She pulled them off and smiled. "May I help you?" she asked.

"Yes, I need to see Dr. Landers."

"Do you have an appointment?"

Tara cuddled Erin's tiny body closer. "No, but it's important. We've come all the way from Phoenix."

The woman glanced at Erin and smiled. "I'll see what I can do."

Matt sat at his desk, going over the report on a child who had been brought into the hospital last week. No matter how many times he'd studied the X rays, it didn't change the fact that the six-year-old boy needed corrective heart surgery.

But the million-dollar question was could the weakened child survive the procedure? And could Matt once again live up to his illustrious reputation and pull off another miracle? He sure as hell hoped so.

The phone rang and he picked it up. "What is it, Judy?"

"I know you're busy, Doctor, but there's a woman with her baby here who wants to see you."

He sighed, knowing his secretary was a pushover. "I'm really busy. Can you make an appointment for her later in the week?"

Judy's voice lowered. "I would, but she came from Phoenix and the baby is only a few months old."

Matt's heart tightened. He knew he couldn't turn away any child, not if there was something he could do. "Okay, send them back."

Matt stood and slipped on his physician's coat, then opened the door just as Judy was escorting the young mother and baby down the hall.

Matt couldn't help but admire the tall attractive woman with short chestnut hair and pale, creamy skin. Her large green eyes were wide-set and slightly tilted at the corners. He glanced at the infant she held so tenderly in her arms. "Hello, I'm Dr. Landers and you're Mrs...."

"*Ms*. Tara McNeal," she corrected. "This is Erin."

Matt motioned for her to go in his office as Judy mouthed a thank-you, then disappeared. "Well, Ms. McNeal," he began as he shut the door. "Have a seat."

She ignored him and looked around the office. After a few seconds, she finally turned her attention to him.

"Can you tell me why it was so imperative I see you?" Matt asked.

"It's about my baby."

"Did my secretary explain I only see patients by referral?" He looked at Erin, then sat behind his desk. "I can send you to an excellent pediatrician, Dr. Talbert."

"No," she blurted, then calmed. "I don't need a pediatrician."

"Then please tell me why you're here." Matt glanced at his watch. He had to talk with Ryan's foster parents. "I have a consultation in a few minutes."

Suddenly Tara wanted to run. She had no doubt she could raise Erin by herself...alone. There was nothing worse than a man who didn't want to be in his child's life.

But she had to keep her promise to Bri.

She stole a glance at the tall Dr. Landers, a good-looking man with a square jaw and a slight cleft in his chin. His wheat-colored hair was parted neatly to one side. Tara swallowed a sudden dryness in her throat when his deep-set coffee eyes settled on her. *Oh, my, sis. You were way out of your league.*

Tara straightened to her full five foot eight. Just think about Erin, she told herself as she saw that the man behind the glass and chrome desk was quickly becoming impatient.

"What was it you wanted to discuss with me, Ms. McNeal?" he asked.

She unfastened the carrier and cradled Erin in her arms. "It's about my sister, Briana...Briana Mc-Neal."

He looked confused. "What about your sister?"

Tara was saddened that he didn't even recognize the name. "She died three months ago. This is her daughter, Erin."

"I'm sorry for your loss," he said. "So you're Erin's guardian now?"

Tara nodded, hoping desperately that would remain true.

"What is your niece's condition?" He stepped around the desk, then reached out and stroked Erin's head. "She looks healthy." He smiled. "But looks can be deceiving, can't they? I really need to see her medical records, though, before I can go any further."

Tara blew out a long breath in frustration. She was tired of his game. "I'm not here because of a medical problem, Dr. Landers. You knew my sister, Briana. You spent time with her over a year ago." She held his gaze. "Erin is your daughter."

Matt Landers stood frozen. This had to be a joke. A bad joke.

"There's been some mistake," he said, trying to remain calm. "I've never met anyone named Briana."

Tara McNeal gave him a knowing look, as if she'd expected him to say exactly that. "Well, according to my sister, you're her daughter's father."

Just the thought of this precious child being his caused a familiar ache in his chest. But there wasn't the remotest possibility of this accusation being true. He shook away the thought and wiped his face of any expression.

"Look, Ms. McNeal, I don't know what kind of scam you're pulling, but I've never met your sister," he insisted.

"Why would my sister lie about this? She was dying." Tara McNeal lowered her tear-glazed eyes.

Matt tried not to notice her tears. "Maybe knowing she was dying, she wanted to make sure her daughter was taken care of."

"I'm taking care of Erin. Besides, I have proof." She maneuvered a large bag off her shoulder, opened it, then took out an envelope. "Explain this," she said, handing it to him.

Matt knew he shouldn't give this woman's claim any credence. All he had to do was show her the door. Or call security. He'd been sought after before. Doctors often had to deal with deluded people. It was the nature of the profession. The price he paid for the acclaim he'd received as a heart surgeon.

But he found himself reaching for the envelope and taking out a birth certificate for Erin Marie Landers. Born March twenty-ninth in Phoenix, Arizona. Mother: Briana McNeal. Father: Dr. Matthew Landers. Suddenly it felt like something was sitting on Matt's chest, and he couldn't breath. He knew it couldn't possibly be true, but to see it on paper... He looked at the rosy-cheeked baby in the woman's arms, and his yearning grew worse.

"Do you still deny you're her father?"

His gaze met Tara McNeal's, but he could not think of anything to say. Then the anger started to build inside his chest as he remembered the years of pain, the anguish he'd gone through.... He shook away the memory. He had to get to the bottom of this. "Your niece is a beautiful child, but she's not mine."

The young woman closed her eyes and drew a long breath.

"Look, Ms. McNeal, I'm sorry, but you have to believe me when I say I never met anyone named Briana McNeal. If I had, why didn't she contact me when she discovered she was pregnant?"

"She did," the redhead insisted. "You talked several times, but then your calls stopped. Then, when she tried to get in touch with you again, your cellular phone conveniently was disconnected.''

Whoever the father was, the guy was a real jerk, Matt thought. ''Then why didn't she call me here at the hospital? You didn't have any trouble finding me.''

Once again he got her icy green-eyed stare. ''She figured you didn't want her around. But in the hospital when she became so sick…'' Tara paused. ''She told me that Erin had a right to know her father.''

Matt rubbed his forehead. Damn. How could this be happening to him? ''Did your sister say where she met me? Was it here in Santa Cruz? Did anyone see us together?''

The baby started to fuss, and Tara shifted Erin to her shoulder. ''According to Briana, the two of you met in Mexico nine months before Erin's birth. She's three months old. That's pretty close to a year ago. Can you tell me that you haven't been to Mexico?''

No, he couldn't. He'd gone to Mexico several times on consultations.

''Of course, I've been there,'' he said. ''I go down to Mexico City for a few weeks every year to perform surgery.'' He raked his hand through his hair. ''But I never leave the hospital except to go to my hotel and sleep.''

There was another flash of pain in Tara McNeal's eyes as she shook her head. ''Okay, I tried. I've come to see you and fulfilled my promise to my sister. But I can't make you want to be a part of your daughter's life,'' she said, wrapping her arms around the baby protectively. ''But don't worry, Dr. Landers, this child won't lack for love. She's got family. *Me*.''

Tara began gathering her bag. "Sorry I bothered you."

Matt drew a long breath. "How many times do I have to tell you, she's not my daughter? So if you're looking for money, you've come to the wrong place—"

Her back straightened. "I didn't come here for your money, Dr. Landers. I already have custody of my niece and I plan to raise her like my own. That means taking full financial responsibility. We're family, and someday she'll have brothers and sisters." Her glare was heated with anger. "But it was Bri's last request that you be told about your daughter."

Matt glanced at Tara's ringless hand. Was she alone? He shook away the feeling of sympathy. She wasn't his problem.

"But you haven't fulfilled your promise, because she's not my child," he said, the words nearly sticking in his throat.

Matt was a man who had always honored his obligations. But this little girl wasn't his. Damn. Damn. Why wouldn't she believe him and leave? "For one last time, I never met your sister."

Just then the baby stirred again and began to cry. He found he wanted to soothe the infant. None of this was her fault, or his. But if Ms. McNeal decided to take this to Riverhaven Hospital's chief of staff, Harry Douglas, it could cause a lot of problems. He'd worked hard to build a career. And what was to keep her from returning years later and doing this again? Whose child was Erin Landers? Surely someone wouldn't go so low as to pretend to be him?

Suddenly a revelation hit him—the key to this mystery. "Wait! Ms. McNeal, I believe I know what happened." He reached for her just as she started for the door. "Please, you can't leave yet."

She jerked out of his grasp. "You finally found your conscience, Doctor?"

"No. Well, yes. Please let me explain. I think I may have some answers for you." He started to speak, but the phone rang. He picked it up. It was Dr. Talbert wondering where he was. He apologized and hung up.

"Look, Ms. McNeal. I have to leave for about thirty minutes. I have an important consultation with a patient. But I'll be back. Please, will you wait?"

"I don't know. Erin needs to be fed."

"Stay here and use my office," he insisted. "Judy can get you whatever you need. Heat the bottle or whatever. Just give me a chance to explain."

She rocked the baby and eyed him suspiciously. "Okay, I'll stay. But only for a short time."

Matt grabbed the folder from his desk and rushed out the door. "Just give me thirty minutes."

Tara watched the man leave. Was this another ploy? She hoped not, but she'd feel better when she and Erin were on their way back to Phoenix. This had been an expensive trip, one she couldn't afford. Now she may have to go home without any answers.

This wasn't the way she'd planned to start her vacation. As a teacher, Tara had the summer off, and she was planning on taking this opportunity to enjoy being a full-time mother. The last few months, she had to ask her neighbor, Mrs. Lynch, to watch Erin while she taught school.

Tara carried her niece to the sofa and opened the diaper bag. She located the bottle she'd prepared at the motel, pulled off the cap, positioned Erin against her and guided the nipple to her tiny mouth.

Tara sat back and tried to relax, but the nagging headache she'd had since last night hadn't gone away. The long drive from Phoenix had been tedious, and they hadn't arrived until late. But it had been thoughts of Bri that had kept Tara awake all night.

Was there more she could have done? Was she the one who had made her sister want to leave home? So many questions, and Tara had no answers, not for herself or for Erin.

Three months ago Tara had gotten a phone call from her younger sister, Briana. It had been nearly three years since their mother's death, when Bri moved out of the family's small rented house in Phoenix. She was only twenty at the time and eager to be on her own.

Many times over the years, she and Bri had argued about her escapades, including the day she left for Los Angeles. Eventually Bri always ended up back home. Not this time, though. Months had gone by before Tara had any idea as to her sister's whereabouts. Then, this past March, she'd gotten a call from Bri announcing she was about to have a baby and needed her.

Without hesitation, Tara had driven the six hours to the shabby apartment in Los Angeles where her sister lived. Shocked at Bri's weak condition, Tara rushed her to a clinic just as her labor began.

It was a difficult birth, but finally the doctor delivered a healthy baby girl by cesarean section. Bri, still weak, developed a strep infection. Complications set in, and…she died three days later.

Tara blinked away tears. No. She couldn't give in

to her emotions. Not now. She had to get through this, to make up for not being there when Bri really needed her.

She looked at the baby asleep in her arms. Now Erin needed her. Tara smiled as she raised her niece to her shoulder and began gently patting her back. A few minutes later, Tara lay her down on the sofa and changed her diaper. Through it all, the baby slept like an angel.

"I promise, I won't leave you," she whispered and covered the sleeping child with a blanket. Tara stood and walked around the spacious ivory-colored room, her shoes sinking into the plush slate gray carpet. Oak file cabinets lined one wall, and a state-of-the-art computer system took up another. The glass and chrome desk was the focal point of the room, placed dramatically in front of the huge picture window. The doctor had done well for himself. Tara remembered reading about the famous pediatric heart surgeon, Dr. Landers, on the Internet. She knew all about him.

At the young age of thirty-eight, Matthew Landers was already one of the top surgeons in the country. He was single, blond, brown-eyed and six feet two inches tall. He loved the beach and golf.

Tara made her way to the window and looked from the third floor on the beautiful California coastline. She drew a breath. "It looks like you have it all, Dr. Landers. Too bad you can't share it with your child."

Suddenly the door to the office opened. The man she'd been thinking about had returned.

Matt came face to face with the attractive Ms. McNeal. Since their meeting, she'd used the baby like a shield, and it was a pleasant surprise to get a look at her attractive slim body. Tall and long-limbed, Tara McNeal didn't lack for curves. She had on a white short-sleeve sweater and a calf-length print skirt, allowing him a glimpse of shapely legs.

Realizing where he was headed, he shook off his wandering thoughts. *Just forget it—the woman can cause you major trouble.* Somehow he was going to convince her that he would never father a child, then abandon her.

Matt glanced toward the sofa. The baby was asleep. "I take it this morning wore her out?" he said as he placed some files on a side table.

"It's her nap time," Tara said. "She should be out for a while."

"Good, that will give us a chance to talk." He motioned to the chair in front of the desk. "Sit down, Tara. May I call you Tara?"

Nodding, she came around the desk and took a seat.

He sat in the chair next to her. "I have an idea as to why my name appears on the birth certificate as Erin's father."

He watched as she folded her arms across her chest. Great, she was already resistant to hearing him out.

"For the past fifteen months," he began, "my life has been turned into chaos because of someone who broke into the surgeon's lounge and stole my wallet from my locker. Not only did he take money and personal pictures—he used my credit card and my identity."

"What does this have to do with my sister?"

He raised his hand. "Just give me a minute. Like

I was saying, this person was acquiring credit cards in my name. I was getting calls about overdue payments, and the hospital administrator received complaints.'' Matt remembered when it started. Harry Douglas had tried to be understanding about the situation, but the administrator's concern was for the hospital's reputation. They couldn't have their top surgeon in financial trouble.

"Believe me, Ms. McNeal, I thought I *had* straightened out the situation. I've always had an impeccable credit rating, but it's a mess now. I couldn't buy a thing. It's still shaky. But I've worked with the police and hired an investigator to catch this guy. Lately things began to quiet down. I thought maybe he had moved on," he said, nodding toward the child. "Until today."

Tara shrugged her shoulders. "And what connection does this have to Erin?"

"I think the same person who used my name to purchase things also…seduced your sister."

Her eyes widened. "If you expect me to believe… That's the craziest story I've ever heard." She tried to stand, and he reached for her hand and stopped her.

Matt paused, feeling Tara's warmth, her softness. Something he hadn't felt in a while. And by the reaction of his body, he realized it had been a *long* while. He released her and leaned back in the chair to refocus. "I know it sounds crazy, but just think about it."

"There's nothing to think about, Dr. Landers. You don't want to be Erin's father. Hey, don't worry about it. Not all men are cut out to be parents. Believe me, my sister and I knew firsthand about an absent dad. And I won't allow Erin to go through the same thing. No father is better than one who's there then disappears.''

Matt had had enough. "If I fathered that child, believe me, I would definitely claim her.''

"Sure. I can see that.''

His frustration grew along with his temper. He got to his feet. "Dammit, woman. I would never abandon a child, because I know exactly what it feels like.''

Tara couldn't move, couldn't breath. She wanted so badly not to believe him. But the look in his dark eyes, the loneliness that showed in the depths of his gaze told her he understood what it was like not to be wanted.

She started to speak, but Matt held up his hand. "Sorry. I guess we need to step back here.'' He did as he suggested and took a calming breath. "I can see my word isn't going to convince you of anything.''

Tara pulled a piece of note paper from her purse and handed it to him. "This is the motel where we're staying. I'm going to be in town until tomorrow. If you decide that you want to be a part of Erin's life, call me.'' She went to the sofa and carefully bundled up her sleeping niece, then gathered her things. She walked out the door wishing that Matt Landers would stop her but also praying that he wouldn't so she could get on with her life. Her life with Erin.

A few seconds later Matt heard the outer office door close. This was a continuing nightmare. He turned to the large window behind his desk. Before him was an incredible view of the Pacific Ocean. Usually after a rough eight-hour surgery or a consultation with parents when he had to tell them bad news, he could find peace and solace in the mesmerizing waves, lose himself in the sound of the rolling surf. None of it helped him now.

The day his damn wallet had been stolen his entire life turned upside down. Matthew James Landers's credit had been shot to hell, and there was next to nothing he could do about it. Damn. It hadn't been enough that the thief used his credit cards, but taking over his identity was worse. Now the man had fathered a child in his name. Matt clenched his fists, fighting anger and…a twinge of envy. He pounded the window frame.

"Hell, is this mess ever going to end?" he asked. Today had been the last straw. And to torment him with a child. That went beyond cruel.

Again his thoughts turned to the pretty woman, Tara McNeal, who'd stood in his office not thirty seconds ago. Damn. Forget her…forget the baby.

*Call your lawyer,* Matt told himself. Let him handle it. But something in those green eyes of hers told him that she was as much a victim as he was. The ironic thing was that Tara McNeal was offering him his heart's desire. The one thing he'd wanted and couldn't have.

A child.

Later that afternoon, Matt heard voices coming from the outer office. He got up and opened the door to find his friend Nick Malone coming down the hall.

"Hey, what brings you here?" Matt asked, grinning.

The dark-haired computer software genius smiled

back. "I wanted to see if you were available for golf Wednesday."

Matt was eager for any distraction. "You know I'm always ready for a game, but since when are you? I believe your exact words were, 'I don't have time to chase around a little white ball.'"

Nick dropped into the chair across from Matt's desk. "I hear the balls come in different colors now."

"Yeah, sure. What's the real reason?"

"It's Cari's idea. She wants me to cut back on my hours at the plant. Take more downtime for myself."

Matt knew Cari Malone well. Before she'd married Nick and given birth to two beautiful children, she had been a nurse on the pediatric floor. One of the best. "So, she still hasn't given up on changing you."

There was a glint in Nick's gray eyes. "And I hope she never does. She and the kids make everything so...perfect."

Matt knew his friend's life had been far from perfect before Cari walked into it and offered her love to Nick and his son, Danny. Love and kids. Something Matt had avoided over the years. His relationships had always been guarded, avoiding anything permanent. Besides, his demanding career made it nearly impossible for him to have a personal life. At thirty-eight, he wished things could be different. A picture of a perky redhead holding a baby flashed in his head. He blinked away the fantasy.

Matt tried to smile but couldn't quite make it, and Nick spotted something amiss right away.

"What's wrong, friend?"

Matt shrugged. "Just a rough day. A new patient, a little boy who has a rough road ahead."

Nick's gaze locked with his. "If anyone can pull it off, you can. You gave Danny a normal life."

Nick's eight-year-old son had had a heart transplant six years ago and had been under Matt's care.

"A lot of factors entered into Danny's recovery and continued good health, including having parents who love him." Matt thought about the baby girl who had been in his office. A child who needed him to be a father. It was too bad that...

Nick's words interrupted his thoughts. "Hey, pal. You sure there isn't anything else on your mind?"

Matt sighed. "This morning I was told I was a father."

## Chapter Two

That evening Tara leaned over the portable baby crib in the corner of the small motel room. Erin had been fed, changed and dressed in her pajamas, and she was finally asleep.

Tara placed a kiss on the baby's rosy cheek, then went to the double bed and sat down. If Erin would sleep a few hours, she could get some rest, too. But Tara doubted she could sleep. Not after what had happened this afternoon. Not after Matthew Landers had denied ever knowing Bri.

Tara rubbed her temples. The headache she'd woken up with still plagued her. She checked her watch. It was getting late, and the good doctor hadn't called. So he didn't care about his own child.

She went into the small kitchenette and located the bottle of aspirin, poured a glass of water and swallowed two tablets.

Tara had had firsthand experience with waiting for a father. Her father hadn't hung around, not for long, anyway. Having a wife and two daughters had been too much for Sean McNeal. He was busy chasing the next big deal. Nothing was going to keep him from what he wanted, not even the responsibility of a family. Sean was going to be rich, he'd told everyone. Even his small daughters had gotten caught up in his crazy dreams until they found out the man was nothing but a fake.

By the time Tara turned fourteen, her dad had disappeared from their lives for good. For months her mother cried, leaving Tara wishing she could help. When her mother had to take on another job to keep the family together, her eldest daughter had been put in charge of watching eight-year-old Briana.

Regret filled Tara. Maybe if she'd done a better job, her baby sister would be alive today. But Bri had always been headstrong. From an early age, she'd had a wild streak. Unlike Tara, she ran after life, and after men, looking for the love their father had denied them.

"I should have been there for you," Tara whispered, believing that Briana left Phoenix because she felt smothered. "I should have gone to visit you. We were family."

Tara had been busy with college and her job, but she could have found time. If only Briana had wanted to see her. Tears stung her eyes. At least in the end, she'd been with Bri. And now that Matt Landers had denied paternity she was going to be Erin's family.

She walked to the crib and gazed at the beautiful baby. She already looked like Briana. The shape of her face and her large eyes were Bri's, although their color was dark brown, like her father's. The wisps of hair that covered her small head were blond. Again like her father. A father who wasn't going to be around.

"I wanted so much for you, sweetie," she whispered, emotion lacing her voice. "But it looks like it's just you and me, Erin Marie. I promise I won't let you down." She took hold of Erin's tiny finger just like she had so many times with Bri. "I double pinky swear. We'll be a family."

There was a soft knock on the door. Wiping away any traces of tears, Tara checked the peephole. Her pulse started to race when she saw Matt Landers. He'd come. She said a quick little prayer and opened the door.

"Can we talk?" he asked.

Tara swallowed. "That depends on what you have to say."

"I believe it's obvious what we have to talk about. The baby. We need to come to a decision that will be the best for all of us."

"You mean that will be best for you," she murmured.

After a few seconds, Tara stepped aside and Matt walked into the small room. He glanced around the standard chain motel surroundings. The double bed with the colorful bedspread. The desk with the menu and coupons from the local restaurant. Then he turned his attention to the baby crib in the corner, and a protective feeling tugged at him.

"Do my accommodations meet with your approval?"

Matt turned to Tara. Faded jeans covered her long, slender legs and accented her narrow waist. A short white T-shirt draped her delicate shoulders and nicely rounded breasts. Her short rust-colored hair was pulled behind her ears. He raised his gaze to her weary green eyes.

"I'm not concerned with your accommodations, Ms. McNeal, just your accusations."

His lawyer, Ed Podesta, had told him he'd handle everything and advised his client to stay away from Tara McNeal and the baby. Even though Matt knew he couldn't possibly be Erin's father, he hadn't been able to stop thinking about her. Her sweet face, her pink cheeks and rosebud mouth. He tended children daily. Many were infants. But he'd never been called a father before. That made little Erin different.

The baby was the innocent one in all this. But was Tara McNeal innocent? "I'm here because there's a child involved. She's the one we have to worry about. Needless to say, you caught me off guard when you came to the office today."

He watched Tara cross her arms.

"I don't want to be the enemy here," Matt continued. "There are some steps we need to take."

"Just what steps are those, Dr. Landers?"

"A blood test."

Early the next day, Tara carried Erin across the medical laboratory parking lot. Matthew Landers was there waiting for her.

The man looked far too good first thing in the morning. He wore a snowy white shirt with dove-gray pleated slacks and expensive black loafers. His hair was perfect, not a strand out of place. Tara found she wanted to mess it up. She quickly pushed away the crazy thought.

He pulled off his dark glasses and squinted into the summer sun. "Good morning, Ms. McNeal," he said.

Tara absently brushed her hair behind her ears, wishing she'd taken time to apply a little makeup. No easy task when she had a baby to care for. "Morning, doctor," she answered.

"Okay, this is a simple test. It could have been done in my office, but..."

Tara straightened. "I know, you want to keep this quiet." She glanced at the small medical building.

She was right, Matt was worried about the gossip that might arise from the test. He didn't want Harry Douglas finding out about this. The hospital grapevine had already built him an impressive reputation as a playboy even though he'd been extremely careful to have kept his personal life private.

"Yes, I'm concerned. I want this matter cleared up. Quickly."

"Why, are you married?"

Matt was surprised by her question. "No, I'm not. But I am a respected doctor in this community." He wouldn't be for long if her accusation became public. He could lose everything he'd worked for. "Are you?"

"Am I what?"

"Married."

"No, but I plan to be someday." She smiled at the baby. "And I'll give Erin brothers and sisters." Matt held open the door to the small medical building, and Tara stepped inside.

Matt wasn't surprised by her answer. Most women, even those with active careers, wanted a family. Something he couldn't offer a wife. "This way,'' he said, directing her down the hall and into the elevator.

They were alone in the small space. He pressed the button for the second floor. As much as he tried not to, he couldn't help but look at the baby. She was awake and alert. Little Erin's arms were waving in the air as her big dark eyes took in her new surroundings. He smiled. She hadn't asked for all this trouble.

He stole a glance at Ms. McNeal. She, on the other hand, was asking for a lot of trouble. If she thought she could come here and bat those big emerald eyes at him... Well, he wasn't going to let her get to him. No matter how soft and touchable her auburn hair looked. He inhaled her soft fragrance, and his stomach tightened.

A chime sounded and the doors opened. He allowed her out first, then directed her down another hall to the lab. Jerry, a golfing buddy and a trusted confidant, was working the early shift and knew they would be coming in. With luck this could be done quickly and privately. In a few hours they'd have the results, and Matt could go on with his life.

He opened the door and stepped aside so Tara could enter, then walked to the deserted counter and rang the bell. The glass window opened, and a middle-aged man with brown hair and a ready smile appeared. ''Hey, Matt, nice to see you.''

They shook hands. ''Jerry. This is Tara McNeal and Erin.''

''Come back to the office,'' Jerry directed. ''We'll do this as quickly as possible.''

Matt stood aside as Tara passed through another door, then paused.

"So how long have you and Jerry been friends?" she asked.

Matt bit back his anger. "If you're insinuating that I'm trying to falsify the blood test, you can forget it. I have a sterling reputation. Or I had, until some bastard stole everything. I want to clear this up more than you know, Ms. McNeal. You have no idea what it's like to have lost this kind of control of your life. I know Erin is not my child, but I'm determined to convince you."

She looked at him for a long moment, then nodded. "Let's do the test."

Two hours later, Tara was in Matt Landers's office, changing Erin's diaper. Crooning to her niece, she was soon rewarded with a smile.

"You were such a good girl," Tara whispered, then placed a kiss on the baby's soft cheek as she managed to get her kicking legs into the stretch suit. Tara took the recently warmed bottle, lifted Erin in her arms, found a spot on the sofa and began feeding her.

She hated hanging around, but the results of the test weren't supposed to take very long. And waiting here was as good as anywhere else. Dr. Landers had given up his office, saying he had a busy schedule of hospital rounds. The receptionist, Judy Shaw, had gone out of her way to be kind, making sure Tara and Erin were comfortable.

All Tara had to do was wait for the test results. Then what? What if Matt Landers had been telling her the truth? What if he wasn't Erin's father? But Bri had sworn she'd only been with one man, Dr.

Matt Landers, head of pediatric cardiac surgery at Riverhaven Hospital.

Her sister's last words echoed in her head. *You've got to find Erin's father. I want him to be a part of her life.*

"Oh, Bri, you always were a dreamer. Just because he fathered a child doesn't mean he wants to be a daddy. Didn't we both learn that the hard way?"

Tara looked at the baby in her arms. "Don't worry, sweetheart. Aunt Tara will always be here for you."

The door opened, and Matt Landers walked in. He wore a white lab coat open over his still snowy white shirt and perfectly pressed trousers. "Jerry faxed me the test results. Do you happen to know your sister's blood type?"

Tara's heart began to pound as she removed the bottle from Erin's mouth, placed the baby against her shoulder and began to gently pat her back. She stood up. "Yes, she's the same as mine, A positive. What are the test results?"

"Inconclusive. It shows I'm O positive. I already knew that, but wanted to redo the test for you. And Erin's results show…she's also O positive."

Tara wasn't sure whether she was happy or not. "So you *are* her father."

Matt Landers didn't show any emotion. "No, I'm afraid that only suggests I *could* be the father. O positive is the most common blood type."

Tara had had enough. If this man didn't want to claim his daughter, she couldn't make him want to be a father. *Sorry, Bri. I tried.* But she was relieved. She could keep sole custody of the baby. "Thank you for your time, Doctor." She walked to the sofa and began gathering her things. The sooner she got out of here the better.

"Where are you going?"

"Back to Phoenix."

"You're not going to try to find Erin's father?"

Tara looked up. "I thought I had found him, but you don't want her."

Matt went to her. "And I told you, I never met your sister, Briana."

"So you keep saying." Tara placed Erin in her carrier.

"But you still don't believe me."

She sighed tiredly. "I don't know what to believe anymore." That much was true. "I'm only doing what I think is best for Erin."

"If you want to do what's best for your niece, stay and help me find the man who's hurt both our lives."

He wanted her to stay? "But what can I do? Bri was the one who knew you...or whoever you say was masquerading as you."

"Please, just stay and talk to the private investigator I've hired."

The phone interrupted him. After a few minutes Matt hung up. "Sorry, that was Harry Douglas, the hospital administrator, reminding me about the big fund-raiser at the end of the month." His dark eyes bore into hers. "That's another reason I want to clear this up. I don't want any bad press coming to Riverhaven."

He sounded so convincing. "I understand that. And I'm not going to make any trouble. I only came to fulfill a promise to my sister." She started to get up. "Now we can all get on with our lives."

He held out a hand to stop her. "But you won't

believe me unless we find the thief. Please, you have to stay.''

''I can't just hang around in a motel room while you try to come up with another story.''

''I told you there isn't another story,'' he argued. ''But this isn't finished. I don't want you coming back in a few years and starting this up again.''

''You think I'd do that?''

His eyes searched hers. ''I'm not sure. I'm not sure of anything anymore.'' He raked his fingers through his hair. ''Look, you don't understand. Riverhaven is a research hospital. We rely heavily on grants and people's generosity. My career started here. I've made a name for myself as a cardiothoracic surgeon. I don't need any scandal.''

Matt walked to the window and looked out. Damn. He hated losing control. And he wasn't about to lose the success he'd worked so hard for. It was unfair. And not just to him, but to the baby. He swung around and stared at Tara. ''Look, we've got to resolve this.''

There was a knock on the door, and a middle-aged man walked in. He was dressed in a pinstripe suit. He had black wavy hair and wore wire-rimmed glasses. His smile was almost a sneer. ''Well, Matt, aren't you going to introduce us?''

''Tara McNeal, this is Ed Podesta…my lawyer.''

''Hello, Ms. McNeal.''

Tara tossed a hurt look at Matt, and he suddenly felt he'd done something wrong.

''Mr. Podesta,'' she said.

Ed dropped his briefcase on the desk and picked up a file. ''These the blood tests?''

Matt nodded. ''They're inconclusive.''

"It doesn't matter," Tara said. "Dr. Landers doesn't want to be Erin's father. And I'm leaving."

"Wait, Tara," Matt called to her. "If you don't stay, you'll always wonder about the truth." He looked at his lawyer for some help.

"And Dr. Landers doesn't need the threat of you showing up later on, claiming paternity."

Tara shook her head. "I told him I wouldn't do that."

"Then extend your stay to allow for one more test."

She frowned. "What test?"

Matt spoke. "There's one test that will prove I couldn't possibly have fathered the child. A DNA test."

Tara blinked. "That's what you're looking for, isn't it? A way to get out of accepting the fact that you're Erin's father."

"I'm not—"

"He's not." Ed Podesta interrupted. "Let me handle this, Matt." The lawyer turned to Tara. "It looks as if Dr. Landers's word isn't good enough for you. And for the future, a DNA test will protect everyone involved."

Tara glanced at Matt. "Don't DNA tests cost a lot?"

"I'll pay."

"But…"

"Look, Ms. McNeal," Podesta began, "Dr. Landers wants to find out who Erin's father is nearly as much as you do. And when the test eliminates him, then perhaps we can find the man who's managed to disrupt several lives."

Tara turned to Matt. Suddenly this all seemed so

sordid, so clinical. But there was a baby involved. She had no choice.

"Are you with me?" Matt asked.

She nodded. "Do we need to go back to the lab?"

Matt turned to Ed. "DNA testing has to be done at a larger facility." He glanced away. "There's another catch. It's going to take awhile to get the results."

"How long?"

"It could take four weeks."

Tara didn't like that. She hoped everything would be straightened out so she could head home. "Okay, we'll do the test and then we'll have to go back to Phoenix. You can call me when the results come back."

"I'd like you and Erin to stay here," Matt said.

Her mouth gaped open. She didn't have the money to stay in Santa Cruz. "There's no way I can afford it. Besides, I don't want to keep Erin in a motel room." She shook her head. "No, it just isn't possible."

Matt nodded. "I understand. But you agree to the test, right?"

"I think it's a good idea."

"And will you talk with the private investigator?" Matt asked.

Tara shrugged. "All right, but I don't think I'll know anything that will help." Good heavens! She was beginning to sound as if she believed his story.

He smiled. "You might be surprised at what you know. Anything your sister told you about the man she knew could possibly help us."

Tara stared at Matt Landers, wondering what he was up to. "Maybe this will all backfire on you."

He glared at her. "Things can't get any worse than they are now."

Tara had agreed to meet in the coffee shop next to the motel that evening with Matt and his private investigator, Jim Sloan. She had fed Erin, and the baby was sleeping peacefully in the carrier beside her in the booth. But for how long? She checked her watch. It was after eight o'clock. Glancing toward the door of the restaurant, she began to think this was a crazy idea.

At a larger, state-of-the-art lab that afternoon, they'd taken blood and saliva samples for the DNA test. Matt had asked that they meet later with Sloan. He wanted to know if she knew anything.

It looked like Dr. Landers wasn't going to show up. She glanced at her watch again. Of course, what did she expect? Since the moment they'd met, he had her jumping through hoops. Well, no more. She wasn't going to wait around for his convenience. She dug through her purse to get some money for her coffee and a tip when she saw him coming toward her.

His steps were hurried as he made his way across the crowded restaurant. Dressed in the same gray slacks and white shirt, he'd added a lightweight jacket to ward off the cool ocean air. He looked slightly rumpled, but that only added to his appeal. The women in the room quickly took notice of the good-looking doctor.

*Stop it!* she told herself. This man had left her sister without a backward glance. Now he was shirking his responsibility with his daughter.

"I'm sorry, Tara," he said, sounding a little breathless. "I had an emergency."

"I wish you'd called." She nodded toward the baby. "Erin needs to go to bed. It's been a long day."

"I know," he said. "I couldn't get to a phone."

Before Tara could say anything more, the waitress appeared.

"I'll have coffee, please," Matt said, then he turned on his killer smile, and the young waitress nearly swooned. Flashes of another charming man came to Tara's mind. Her father. She swiftly pushed away the thought.

"Look," she said, "it's late, and I don't want Erin to wake up in the middle of your investigator asking me questions."

"I know, and I apologize for keeping you both here, especially since Jim Sloan is still in Los Angeles following up on a lead." He glanced around. "But there is someone else who might convince you that my story isn't crazy."

Tara didn't care if he was about to introduce her to the president, she wasn't going to hang around. She felt that was all she'd been doing the past forty-eight hours. "Why don't you let me return to Phoenix? I promise I'll never contact you again."

His eyes narrowed, but he kept silent until the waitress brought his coffee and left. He leaned forward. "And you'll always wonder if I'm the baby's father. What are you going to tell her when she grows up? That her father, Dr. Matt Landers, didn't want her? No, I'm through being a pawn for this other guy."

Tara saw an anger in his eyes she hadn't seen be-

fore. Not that she was afraid, but she suspected he
was a dangerous man to cross. She raised her chin.
"Then what do you want from me?"

Matt's gaze went to the door, then he suddenly
stood. "I'll be right back." He walked to a middle-
aged man in a dark suit and shook his hand. Together
they came to the table. Matt slid into the booth, and
the man followed.

"Tara, this is Detective Tom Warren with the
Santa Cruz Police Department. Tom, this is Tara
McNeal." He pointed to the carrier and the sleeping
child. "Her niece, Erin."

Detective Warren reached into his jacket pocket
and pulled out a small leather folder containing a
badge. "Ms. McNeal. Nice to meet you." He smiled,
and lines crinkled around his kind hazel eyes. "Cute
baby."

A little nervous, Tara examined the silver shield.
"Why are you here, Detective?"

"Dr. Landers called today and asked me to talk
with you."

"About what?"

"I was the one who answered the call at Riverhaven Hospital when a robbery took place in the doctor's lounge. Dr. Landers's locker had been broken
into. The thief got away with his watch and wallet.
Then the doctor and I met again a few months later.
He came into the station after he discovered someone
was using his name on credit applications. He filed
a fraud complaint.

"Since then, I've been putting in extra time trying
to catch this guy. Whoever he is, he's been pretty
slick so far. I can't decide if the guy is just brazen,
or if he's got a vendetta against the doctor."

"Dr. Landers is lucky to have inspired your dedication."

Tom Warren smiled. "The whole department is trying their best. A few years back, Dr. Landers operated on my partner's little boy. My godchild. We take care of our own here in Santa Cruz."

Tara looked at Matt. Was he really everything that he seemed to be? Could a man who'd spent his career saving children abandon his own? She wanted to think no.

"But until this last year," the detective continued, "there weren't any laws to protect against this crime. Believe me, when this guy is caught, we're going to throw the book at him. Sorry to say, we've had leads but nothing has panned out." The officer drew in a long breath and relaxed against the back of the booth. "I'm sorry, Ms. McNeal, I know you want this man for purely different reasons, but if you have any information that might help us we'd be anxious to hear it."

"All my sister told me about the man was his name... Dr. Matthew Landers."

"If you can think of anything else please stop by the station." He pulled out a business card. "I'm usually there during the day." He slid out of the booth.

"I'll be leaving tomorrow, Detective." There was no reason for her to stay. She doubted that even the sainted Matt Landers could get the police to lie for him.

He wasn't Erin's father.

"Well, I've got to go," the detective said.

"Thanks for coming by, Tom," Matt said. He stood and shook the officer's hand.

"No problem." He nodded to Tara and left.

Tara started gathering her things. She hated to be wrong, but the facts were pretty daunting. "I guess that means I'm heading back to Phoenix. I'm sorry I disrupted your life, Doctor."

"My life was a mess long before you came," he said. "But you can actually help me. We can still help each other."

"I doubt that," she said skeptically.

"No, really. This could be an opportunity to find the man who's destroying my life, and more importantly, who ran out on your sister."

She closed her eyes and sighed. "I told you I've taken responsibility for Erin, and I will raise her."

"So you believe me? You finally believe that I never knew your sister—that I'm not Erin's father?"

She almost wished he were. Now she had to deal with the fact that her niece's father was not only a jerk, but a thief, too. "I believe you."

He smiled, reached across the table and took her hand. "Then stay and we'll work together to find him."

She was weakening and she hated that. But she had promised Bri. "What about the DNA test? It's costing you a lot of money."

He shook his head. "It's worth it. And it doesn't hurt to have the proof, anyway."

Tara knew that he was talking about her. She stood and picked up the carrier. "Well, Doctor, I hope everything works out for you."

He stood, too. "So you are leaving?"

"I've got to get home." She didn't have money to throw away on motels and restaurant food.

"But I still need your help. Can't you stay just a few more days and talk with Jim Sloan?"

"Look, this trip has been expensive—"

"Then let me take care of things for the next few days," he offered.

She shook her head. No handouts. "That won't be necessary." She started across the room. Matt tossed some bills on the table and followed her out the door.

He silently walked with her across the parking lot to the motel. Finally he spoke. "Look, I know these last few months have been hard on you. Your sister's death had to be a shock, and taking care of a baby has to be difficult for a single mother."

She stopped suddenly, and he nearly ran into her. "What are you getting at, Doctor? Are you trying to say I can't care for my own flesh and blood?"

"No, of course not. But what are you going to do in years to come when little Erin starts asking questions? What are you going to tell her about her father? And what about Briana? You said it was her dying wish that you find her daughter's father."

Tara closed her eyes. "I tried, but you're not...him."

"So you're going to quit?" He stepped closer, his eyes dark and compelling. "Stay, Tara, and together we can find this man. I can put a stop to the trouble he's causing me, and you can fulfill your promise to your sister. Then move on and be Erin's mother."

Tara sighed. She was having a hard time telling this man no. She couldn't think of a logical argument to his suggestion. "Okay, I'll stay—just until I've talked to the private investigator."

## Chapter Three

Late the next afternoon, Matt checked his rearview mirror to see Tara's white compact following him. It took a lot of convincing, but she'd finally agreed to speak with the PI.

Matt settled in his seat as he drove through town. He liked this long, peaceful drive home. Heading up the Coast Highway, he caught a glimpse of the magnificent sunset over the Pacific Ocean. Only in California could you get such a beautiful view.

After medical school he'd applied to hospitals on the west coast. He ended up doing his internship and surgical residency at the University of San Francisco Hospital. He had been raised in Ohio and had been immediately seduced by the warmer year-round climate, but the ocean was his true love. After paying off his school loans and accepting a job at Riverhaven, he bought a condo with an ocean view. A few years back, he decided he wanted a house. His own private strip of beach. A home that would be far away from his demanding career—a place where he could find peace and solitude.

But there'd been very little peace for the past two days.

Just twenty-four hours ago he and little Erin had given blood and saliva samples. It wasn't going to help. Of course, his lawyer had advised that a little insurance was imperative to keep him out of a paternity suit.

Matt recalled Tara's words from last night. ''I'll never contact you again,'' she'd said convincingly. But Matt knew he was in a vulnerable position. Just the fact of his being a much publicized surgeon in the community made him an easy target.

But he'd gotten a reprieve when Tara agreed to stay in town awhile. Matt wasn't completely confident that she wouldn't cause trouble. And now Tara and Erin were going to be closer than ever, invading his private territory, coming to his home.

Checking in his rearview mirror, he saw that Tara was still in his sights. He put on his turn signal and pulled off the highway onto a narrow winding road. He passed a few of his neighbors, their homes secluded from view of the road by trees and overgrown shrubs and vines. That was the reason people bought here—the solitude.

He reached the end of the road and the wrought-iron gate with the fuchsia-colored bougainvillea woven through the bars, nearly hiding the one-story brick and stucco structure behind it. He pressed the button overhead, and the electronic gate opened. Driving up the brick driveway, he hit another button.

The garage door raised, and he parked his car in one of the three spots.

Matt climbed out, and the compact pulled up in the driveway. He waited as Tara got out, then went to help her with the baby. Their hands touched accidentally as he reached for the diaper bag, and she jumped. His skin tingled.

"Sorry, I wanted to help."

"Thank you. I'm used to doing for myself."

He couldn't help but sense her uneasiness. He didn't blame her. She must feel like she was being kidnapped. But he had to clear his name.

After she gathered the baby, Matt escorted her through the garage and into the house. They went through a spacious utility room, then continued into the large kitchen. The cabinets were whitewashed and the tiled countertops were Wedgwood blue. The spicy aroma of enchiladas baking in the oven teased his nose and made him smile. Juanita had made his favorite. His housekeeper for the past three years probably had gone all out when he'd called her earlier and announced he was bringing home a female guest for dinner.

"Juanita," he summoned. "Where are you?"

"Just hold your horses," the housekeeper exclaimed as she entered the kitchen. "So, you finally made it."

Matt smiled at the woman in her late fifties. She had salt and pepper hair pulled into a bun. Still trim, she wore dark slacks and a white blouse.

Juanita only had eyes for the guests. "Welcome." She went to Tara and shook her hand, then glanced at the baby. "Oh, my goodness, isn't she adorable?"

As if she understood, Erin began kicking her legs, waving her arms and making cooing sounds.

Tara set the carrier on the kitchen table and allowed the two to get to know each other.

"If you'd like, Juanita can watch Erin while you talk with the investigator."

Tara's green eyes darted from the baby to him. She was unable to hide her apprehension.

Matt went to the table and picked up the carrier. "Erin can go with us. Juanita, you can spoil her later." Matt handed the carrier to Tara.

After a moment's hesitation, Tara set Erin on the table. "I'm sorry, I guess I'm a little overprotective."

"You can't be too careful these days," the housekeeper announced. "I have three grandchildren myself. I worry all the time."

"Just don't spoil her too much," Tara warned.

The older woman grinned brightly. Matt knew the request would be ignored.

"Come with me, please," he said.

Tara nodded and wondered what had possessed her to agree to come here. Despite Dr. Landers's glowing reputation at the hospital, she didn't really know the man. One thing was for sure, they both needed answers to this puzzle. Maybe together they could locate the mystery man who had taken over Dr. Matthew Landers's name...and fathered Erin.

Tara followed Matt into a large dining room. The walls were painted light cream, and the sand-colored plush carpeting was soft under her feet, a beautiful contrast to the mahogany table and chairs polished to a high gloss. A hutch with cut-glass doors was filled with china and crystal. She glanced toward the living-room area. A sectional sofa sat in front of the fireplace along with a glass-topped coffee table on which expensive-looking figurines rested. But it didn't look like anyone spent much time in here. What a shame not to enjoy the incredible view of the ocean through the huge picture window.

Tara turned to Matt. His piercing brown gaze was on her. His unspeaking eyes prolonged the moment just enough to spark an awareness. Finally she looked away and drew a breath. When she turned back, Matt had started down the hall. She hurried and caught up with him at a set of double doors. He pulled them open and walked into the den.

Tara's gaze moved to the bookcases that took up one wall. Besides tons of medical books, there was a high-tech stereo system that probably required a degree in electronics to operate. Next to the bookcase sat a camel-colored leather sofa. On the opposite wall was a huge stone fireplace with a pair of very old golf clubs mounted on the face.

She walked to a set of French doors that led outside to a weathered deck and the backyard. Beyond a rise she could hear the ocean surf.

"You have a beautiful home."

He stepped behind the desk. "Thank you. I spend most of my time in this room when I'm home."

"I can understand why," she said, imagining a blazing fire on a cold evening, soft music in the background and Matt sipping a glass of wine.

The doorbell rang, and Matt went to answer it.

Tara looked through the French doors. The lawn was a lush green and well cared for. About fifty yards across the grass toward the ocean, perched close to the bluff, was a pewter-colored cottage with burgundy trim. She smiled. It looked like a little gingerbread house.

She wandered to the mantel and glanced at the photographs, one of an elderly couple and a blond-haired boy. The towheaded Matt Landers looked to be about fourteen. He was tall and gangly and wore glasses. Who would have thought he'd turn out to be so handsome? Tara quickly turned her focus to other pictures of Dr. Landers and children. Who were they? Nieces, nephews, maybe patients?

She heard voices and returned to the sofa as a man followed Matt into the room.

"Tara, this is Jim Sloan, the investigator I told you about," Matt said.

The investigator was in his mid-thirties and dressed in a sport shirt and dark trousers. He had brown hair that was a little long but neatly combed.

"Hello, Mr. Sloan," Tara said.

"Please call me Jim. And may I call you Tara?" he asked as he pulled a chair toward the sofa. "I want to apologize for not being here sooner. I was delayed down south."

She nodded.

"Well, Tara, as the doctor must have told you, I need to ask you some questions. So the sooner we get on with this, the faster we may be able to find this man." He pulled a notebook from his pocket. "Can you tell me where your sister, Briana, met *her* Dr. Landers?"

Tara exchanged a nervous glance with Matt. "She just said she met him in Mexico when she went there on vacation with a friend."

"Did she call the man she met by name?"

"She told me his name was Matt Landers and he was a heart surgeon."

Jim took some notes. "What friend went with her?"

Tara shrugged. "I'm not sure. Bri and I hadn't been in touch much the past year. I didn't know she was pregnant until she called two days before she delivered Erin. No one else came to visit Bri in the hospital."

Matt watched sadness veil Tara's features and knew this situation had to be hard on her. "Maybe the friend moved away," he said.

"L.A. is a big city," Jim said. "A person could get lost there. Do you have any idea who this friend is?"

"I can only tell you she moved to L.A. with Cathy Guthrie. I remember Bri telling me that Cathy got married to a Marine her first year here in Los Angeles. Then she and her husband moved to San Diego."

"Do you think she and your sister kept in touch?"

"I don't know."

Matt watched as Tara brushed wisps of auburn bangs from her forehead, her eyes showing deep concentration. He knew she was trying hard to remember.

"What about in your sister's apartment?" Jim continued writing. "Did she have anything belonging to Matt Landers?"

Tara didn't want to go through this—airing private family matters in front of strangers. She and Bri hadn't had the best relationship over the years, and it hurt to share how badly she'd failed her sister. "I didn't find much, just her clothes, a little jewelry..."

She suddenly remembered something. "Wait, there was a ring. Bri wore an emerald ring. It was rather pretty, but she kept twisting it around her finger whenever she talked about Matt."

Matt's expression never wavered.

"Did she say where she'd gotten it?" the investigator asked.

Tara shrugged. "No, but when packing up her things, I found a velvet box. I saved it…for Erin." She wanted to give her something of her mother's.

"Was there a name on the box?"

She sighed. "I'm not sure. Why is this important?" She looked at Matt. His dark eyes were intense. One brow was arched.

"Because, Tara, if we have the jeweler's name maybe he'll remember who bought the ring and what the person looked like. It's a long shot, but it's all we have right now."

She nodded. "My neighbor has my house key. I could have her look for me."

Matt rewarded her with a smile, and an odd feeling gripped Tara's stomach. "That would be great," he said.

"Could she look for an address book, too?" Sloan said. "Maybe this Cathy Guthrie is in there, or other friends who might have gone with her to Mexico."

"Okay. Anything else?" She wanted the interrogation over.

"What was your sister's last address?"

It had been nothing more than a small room in a house in a graffiti-filled neighborhood, but Tara gave it to him. "But Bri had lived other places. She must have moved there when she had to quit working because of complications with the pregnancy. She had to stay in bed the last three months.''

''Why didn't she go home to Phoenix?'' Jim asked.

Guilt and shame filled Tara. Her throat tightened, making it difficult to speak. ''Bri and I hadn't been close…in a long time, not since our mother died….'' She looked away, not wanting to see a judgmental look.

''How long did Bri live in L.A.?''

''Over three years.''

''So you didn't know about her life? Her job…the men…''

''Look, my sister and I may not have seen eye to eye on everything, but I loved her. And pregnant or not, Bri was family. And when she told me Matt Landers was Erin's father, I took it as the truth.'' She could feel the tears building, but she wouldn't cry in front of strangers. That she'd do in private.

Matt reached out and covered her hand with his. ''I'm sorry, Tara.'' He glared at Sloan. ''We have no right—''

No matter how comforting his touch was, she pulled away. ''That's right, you don't.''

Jim wasn't apologetic at all. He forged ahead. ''Okay. I have one more question, then we'll stop. When was Bri in Mexico?''

''Bri said she went to Acapulco the last week of May a year ago. She met a man named Matt Landers the next day by the hotel pool.'' Tara tried to control the heat creeping up her neck, recalling her sister's all-too-vivid description of the good doctor and their heated sexual affair.

She studied Matt. Although he hadn't been her sister's lover, Tara couldn't stop the images of this man's probable sexual prowess. She jerked her head toward Jim. "They had a two-week affair that was supposed to continue after returning home."

"How old was your sister?"

"Twenty-three."

"My God, that would make me fifteen years her senior." Matt's expression became angry as he stood and paced. "She was hardly more than a child."

"Bri could make herself look a lot older," Tara said, remembering in high school how Bri and her friends would dress up. With her shapely body, people couldn't believe she was only seventeen.

"Do you have a picture?" the investigator asked.

Tara opened her purse and pulled out her wallet. She flipped through the photos until she came up with the last one Bri sent their mother. "It's one of those glamour shots. My sister was naturally pretty, though."

Matt took the picture and examined the striking blue-eyed blonde closely.

"Bri was given the looks in the family. She's the image of our mother," Tara said.

"She's beautiful," Matt said, then glanced at Tara. "You look alike. Only your coloring is different."

Tara blushed, knowing there had been several differences. Body type, for one. Bri was shapely where Tara was thin. Bri's eyes were sparkling blue to Tara's hazel green. Bri was outgoing and could draw any man's attention. Tara was shy and wasn't comfortable in crowds.

Matt handed the picture back to Tara. "I might have been in Mexico City during that time, but I never met this woman."

Jim Sloan studied his notes, then turned to Matt. "I'm beginning to think this is personal, that this guy is out to intentionally ruin you and your reputation."

Matt sat in the den and stared out the window at the roaring surf. He took a drink from his long-neck bottle of beer. He'd made an attempt to eat, but after Tara refused to stay he didn't feel much like food. Not even Juanita's enchiladas.

"Dammit. Why does everything have to be so complicated?"

"If you're talking about a woman, it comes with the territory."

Matt swung around to find Nick Malone standing in the doorway. "Nick." Matt walked across the room to welcome his friend. They shook hands.

"Juanita let us in." He held up a beer. "She's even taken care of us with a selection from the bar."

"Us?"

Nick's wife, Cari, peeked in. "You guys talking about me?" she asked with a smile that lit up her bright blue eyes.

Matt smiled as the petite blond woman came over and hugged him. Dressed in jeans and an ivory sweater, she looked about sixteen.

"This is a pleasant surprise," he said.

"Sure. Everyone loves people to just drop in," she said.

Matt never minded the Malones dropping by. He'd always considered Nick and Cari close friends. Nick knew nearly everything about him, from his childhood to his disastrous relationship with his ex-fiancée. And Cari had worked for him at the hospital for a short while until she found Nick. Matt had watched the two fall in love, had even helped the relationship a little.

"What's the occasion that's brought you two out of the house without the kids?" Matt asked.

Nick took a drink of his beer, then said, "I thought my wife needed a night out. I kidnapped her for a quiet dinner at the Sandy Cove Restaurant down the road. But if we'd known Juanita was making her enchiladas, we would have come here instead."

"You know you don't need an invitation."

"Even when you have a woman over?" Nick said as he came up behind his wife, slipped his arms around her waist and locked his fingers together. After being married for nearly five years, they still couldn't keep their hands off each other.

Matt felt the heat rise in his face. "I take it Juanita just happened to mention Tara to you."

"Well, not all the details," Cari said, her eyes sparkling with curiosity. "I was hoping you would fill us in." She held up her hand. "Or you can just tell us that it's none of our business."

Matt saw the eager look on Cari's face and had to smile. He knew for certain that whatever he said to them would never go any further.

"Is this the same woman who's accused you of being her niece's father?" Nick asked.

Matt had no doubt that his friend would have told his wife the whole story. "Her name is Tara McNeal, and now thanks to Detective Warren, she finally believes that I never had an affair with her sister. This afternoon we met with Jim Sloan, the investigator I've had working on this case."

"Could she help with any information?" Nick asked.

"Some. But it seems like the guy who's doing this knows my every move. He was in Mexico seducing Briana McNeal when I was there teaching my surgical procedures."

The Malones exchanged a look, then Cari spoke. "Maybe there's someone who wants to cause you trouble."

"I can't imagine who," Matt said, trying to think of anyone he'd alienated enough to want to destroy his life.

Nick and Cari sat on the edge of the sofa, and Cari looked up expectantly. "It's hard to believe that someone fathered a child just to get back at you."

Matt had to agree with her. "I think this guy just found it convenient to seduce a woman using my name."

"Can we do anything?" Cari asked. "I could tell Tara all your good qualities."

Nick stood. "No, Matt should stay clear of the woman and let his lawyer handle it."

Matt didn't say anything. He didn't want to tell them that he'd already ignored his lawyer's advice. "I can't. Tara might be able to help me find the man impersonating me."

"All this has got to be hard on her, too," Cari said, "Especially after losing her sister so recently and now having the responsibility of a baby."

A pain tore at Matt's chest. No one ever thought about how this affected the child. "The baby isn't mine."

Cari smiled. "I know you would never walk away from your child, Matt. I take it you're running a blood test?"

Matt nodded again. "Since we're both O positive,

my lawyer suggested a DNA test, just for insurance.'' He sighed tiredly, thinking about the hospital administrator. ''If Harry finds out he won't be too happy about the news.''

''No, he won't,'' Cari agreed. ''Especially with the hospital's charity auction coming up in a month.'' Surprisingly, she laughed. ''It would be fun just to see his face when he heard about—''

''No!'' Matt almost shouted. ''I don't want any of this to get out. It's bad enough my credit is in a shambles. My career is too important to me.'' It was the only thing he had in his life.

Nick stepped in. ''Hey, you don't have to worry about Harry and your job at Riverhaven. Hell, Dad's money nearly built the heart wing, and I can just as easily stop any future donations.''

Cari patted her husband's arm. ''Don't worry, honey, Harry isn't going to do anything crazy. He needs Matt more than Matt needs him.''

Right now, Matt had more to worry about than his own skin. ''We have to think about the innocent baby in all this. She's the one who'll be hurt. Damn this jerk for causing these problems.'' And for causing him to long for something he could never have.

''Then just sit tight for awhile,'' Nick said. ''You'll be cleared of everything. And your life can get back to normal.''

Matt didn't know if he wanted his life normal again. The memory of Tara McNeal's face wasn't going to go away easily, nor was the thought of having a child. Forgetting them might take a lifetime.

It was nearly ten o'clock when Matt knocked on Tara's motel room door. He knew it was late, but he couldn't take the chance and wait until tomorrow. She could be gone by then.

"Who is it?" Her voice was muffled through the door.

"It's Matt...Matt Landers."

The door opened slightly, and Tara's face appeared, her short hair mussed. She was wearing an oversize T-shirt. Damn, she'd been asleep. He blinked away the picture of her curled up in bed.

"May I come inside and talk to you?"

Tara opened the door, and he stepped inside.

The first thing he saw was the bed. The sheets were rumpled, and the pillow had an imprint where Tara had lain her head.

"I'm sorry I woke you." He turned to look at her. A big mistake. Her T-shirt might have been oversize, but there was plenty of leg revealed. Long, gorgeous leg. "But I...I wanted to make sure I saw you before you left. I wanted to thank you for talking with Jim Sloan." He glanced around nervously. "And I was hoping to give it one more shot and try to convince you to stay."

Having Matt in her room made Tara nervous. She grabbed her cotton robe from the end of the bed and slipped it on. "I told you earlier, I can't. It's best that I take Erin back to Phoenix."

"And what? Wait?" he asked. "I thought you wanted to find her father." He went to the baby's bed and glanced at Erin. She was asleep on her side, her little mouth moving occasionally in a sucking motion. He moved away from the crib.

"She's a beautiful child," he said.

Tara nodded. She was confused by this man. He seemed to have everything. A successful career, money, a beautiful home. But she'd caught a twinge of loneliness in his eyes that mirrored hers. "You would think any man would want her." Tara hadn't realized she'd spoken until she saw Matt tense.

"Then don't give up on finding her father."

"I'm not giving up. I loved my sister," she whispered tersely as she fought the tears flooding her eyes. "I would have done anything for her, and I'll do anything for Erin. But I don't have the time or the money to run around the country."

"Stay in Santa Cruz, and we'll find out the truth together," he challenged.

She didn't want to argue with this man, not anymore. Not to mention she was half-dressed. Nervously she tucked her hair behind her ear. "I can't—"

"Yes, you can. What's to stop you?"

Tara turned away. "I have a home, a job and a life, Dr. Landers. I can't just drop everything." Her biggest problem was the good-looking man standing too close. Making her want things that she only dreamed about. She couldn't let herself depend on him, lean on him. He could hurt her and Erin with his good looks and easy charm. The type of man who made her feel things... She pushed away the thought. No, she was safer back home.

The phone rang, and Tara hurried to pick it up before it woke the baby. "Hello."

"Tara." The familiar voice of her Phoenix neighbor came across the line.

"Mrs. Lynch. Is there something wrong?" Tara asked as she turned away from Matt.

"No, child," the sixty-year-old woman said. "I wanted to let you know that I sent off the things you asked for. Your sister's things, the black address book and jewelry box.''

"Thank you, Mrs. Lynch. You've helped so much."

"Well, I want to help. I know this has been a rough time for you and the little one. Just don't worry about the house, I'll take care of things here."

Tara smiled at the woman's kindness. The small, two-bedroom house Tara rented was the same stucco structure she and Briana had lived in all their lives. And Mrs. Lynch had been her neighbor all that time. "I appreciate that so much. Erin and I will be home in a few days."

She heard a deep sigh on the line. "Well, that is good news. I sure miss that little girl. How is she doing? I bet she's grown."

"I'll let you measure her when we get back." She glanced at Matt. "I better go. Thank you for all your help. Goodbye." She hung up the phone.

She rose and crossed the room to where Matt was waiting. "That was my neighbor in Phoenix. She found the address book and jewelry box. She sent them off today. You should have them in a couple of days."

"Good. After Jim goes over them, I'll make sure he returns your property. Just give me your address." He cocked an eyebrow. "Unless you're going to take me up on my offer to stay until either we get this thing solved or you have to start back for the new school year."

She studied him for awhile and fought taking him up on the offer. She shook her head. "I can't."

His look of disappointment surprised her. Tara knew she should just go home and call him with the information, but she had to admit she was curious, and that was dangerous. "Why do you want us to stay?"

Matt shrugged. "First, I want to find the man who stole my name. And you might remember something your sister told you that could help us. So, if you think I'm grasping at straws, maybe I am. I'm grasping at anything to get my life back." He shot a glance at the crib. The longing in his eyes gripped her heart. "And for the baby's sake, too. I know what it's like to be abandoned."

All the way home in the car, Matt cursed himself for revealing so much. Tara McNeal didn't need to know about his past. No one did.

He'd always been a private person. He'd grown up an only child, adopted by an older couple who'd waited years for a baby. So he'd been on display all the time, something he hated. He'd been a shy kid, had trouble making friends. In high school, he tried sports but was growing so fast his coordination was almost nonexistent. So he spent his evenings at the library, studying. He strove to excel, to be as good as he could be. To be awarded a scholarship to a prestigious college and medical school.

But in the back of his mind, what had always driven him was the fact that his birth mother had rejected him. A familiar tremor surged through him, making him feel isolated and vulnerable. He'd never forget the questions that had haunted him as a child. What had been the imperfection in him that made his mother discard her newborn son in a bus station rest room? Matt gripped the steering wheel tighter and cursed. Why was he thinking about this now? He had come to terms with his past long ago. Immediately a picture of little Erin came into his head.

And along with the baby came the beautiful aunt. Was that the reason he wanted Tara McNeal to stay?

He groaned. He was doing exactly what Ed Podesta advised him not to do. Was he insane? Or just so lonely that he wanted to spend time with the woman? But why Tara McNeal? She wasn't even his type. What was his type? Any woman who didn't get too close or want a permanent relationship.

Matt's demanding career always came first, and that didn't leave him much time for a personal life, he thought as he drove his car off the highway onto the narrow road. That had been the choice he'd made years ago.

He thought back to when he'd been accepted as a surgical resident at San Francisco University Hospital, his first time on the West Coast and the first time he'd ever fallen in love.

Matt drove through the gate and parked in the garage. He got out but instead of going inside walked around to the back of the house. The cool breeze was refreshing but didn't wash away the memories. Memories he'd pushed aside for years while he built his career as one of the best pediatric heart surgeons on the coast.

But after meeting Tara and Erin, he realized how vulnerable he was to his past…and to his own human flaws.

Would his life have taken a different turn if Julie, the woman he'd fallen in love with in medical residency, hadn't left him?

He crossed the lawn to the bluff. The cool evening breeze brushed against his skin as he looked down the five-foot drop to the surf. The crashing waves were loud, but the rhythmic movement had always been soothing to him.

Matt shut his eyes and thought about the baby he'd seen in the crib tonight. Every time he picked up a child, held one, performed delicate surgery on their precious bodies, his pain only grew. The pain and loneliness in his heart never went away. He knew that being adopted added to his emotional inadequacies. The constant desire to know where he'd come from...and the knowledge that he would never leave a part of himself behind in a child.

The wind whipped through his hair as he looked at the high surf, listened to the waves crashing against the rocky coast. "Dammit, this isn't fair." An ache constricted his chest. Life was too cruel. He'd gladly claim the child the father didn't want.

But Matt knew that it was impossible. Because of a case of mumps during adolescence, he was essentially sterile. He drew a shaky breath.

He could never claim any child.

## Chapter Four

At one-fifteen the following afternoon, Matt collapsed in the chair behind his desk. This was the first chance all day he'd had to take a break.

He'd been going strong since seven. First stop, he'd gone over procedure with his surgical team before his eight o'clock surgery. By eleven, he had completed a successful heart valve replacement, and the six-year-old patient was in recovery.

After spending the next hour monitoring the boy, Matt was grateful he could go to the parents and give them optimistic news about their son's progress. As he watched the boy's mother sit beside her child's bed and hold his hand, his thoughts turned to Tara and Erin.

Had they left town? Was she going to be able to get all the way back to Phoenix without car trouble? He quickly reminded himself she wasn't his concern anymore and went to do rounds. Again at eleven-thirty thoughts of Tara distracted him from his consultation, and he finally took solace in his office.

His stomach growled and he decided that the sandwich Judy brought him from the cafeteria looked pretty good. He took a bite of the turkey on whole wheat. Not bad. He finished half before he heard a knock on the door.

Cari Malone walked in. "Sorry, I didn't mean to interrupt your lunch. I can come back later if it would be better."

Matt got up. "My day is only going to get worse," he said as he offered her a seat. He smiled at the pretty woman who was a good friend. Funny, he'd never thought that it was possible to have a woman for a friend until he met Cari. "Does your husband know you're meeting another man?"

She winked as she sat down in the chair in front of the desk. "I told him it was business." She reached into her folder and pulled out a notebook.

Matt groaned. "Oh, no, not the—"

"The Riverhaven Annual Charity Ball," she said. "And don't go running for the door. I have Judy posted outside."

"Just so you know, no matter what you say, I'm not going to be raffled off again. I don't care how much money it brings in."

Cari raised a hand. "Now, calm down. You're safe this year."

"You've said that before," he murmured.

She pretended to be irritated. "Boy, you and Nick are so suspicious."

"With good reason."

"You have to admit we did make a lot of money. But this year the committee decided to do a silent auction. And we've already been given several great prizes. I was just going to ask you to be one of the announcers."

Matt eyed the petite blonde closely. There had to be a catch. This was too simple. "I guess I can help out, as long as I'm not going to be—in any way, shape or form—on the auction block."

Cari's blue eyes twinkled. "Your bod is safe for another year."

"Then I'll volunteer, but only to help with promoting the auction, nothing more."

She sighed. "You're a spoilsport. We're trying to make money here. And as one of the few single doctors around, not to mention good-looking, you should know we have to use your talents the best way we can."

Matt found himself laughing. "Then how about we raffle off my surgical abilities?"

Her eyes lit up again. "Now, that might work. Too bad you aren't a plastic surgeon."

"Cari, I mean it." He shook a finger at her. "I want no surprises on this."

"A few surprises might liven up your life. Speaking of which, how are Ms. McNeal and her niece?"

Now what brought that up? Matt wondered as he shook his head. "As far as I know she's on her way back to Phoenix."

"I take it she finally believed you."

He nodded. "And things are moving forward with the case. Jim is in Mexico, checking out some hotels."

She smiled. "Good. I bet in no time they'll find this guy and things will get back to normal."

Matt doubted that, but he wasn't just talking about his credit rating. He couldn't help but think about Tara…and Erin. He shook away his wayward thoughts and said, "Yeah, but it may take years to clear up this mess. I've already spent thousands of dollars trying to find this guy."

"Hey, I can still put you up for auction. I might just find you the *rich* woman of your dreams."

Matt glanced away. He had stopped looking for the woman of his dreams because he could not provide her with everything she would need—a family. "I'm getting too set in my ways. Just ask Juanita. No one could put up with me."

Before Cari could argue the point, the phone rang.

"Excuse me." Matt picked up the receiver. "Dr. Landers."

"Matt, this is Ben Hall down in emergency."

Matt tensed hearing the emergency room doctor's voice. His call usually meant a new patient for him. "What's up, Ben?"

"We have someone down here who asked me to call you. A Tara McNeal."

Matt tensed. "What happened? Is it her baby?"

"No, her baby is fine. But the mother has a severe laceration on her hand. She asked that you be notified."

Tara was hurt. What next? "I'll be right down." He hung up and stood. "Tara's in emergency." He rushed out the door, not surprised to find Cari on his heels.

* * *

Tara could hear Erin crying. "I need to go to my baby," she told the nurse.

"In a minute. The doctor has to look at you."

Tara winced at the pain shooting through her hand. Not only did she hurt, but she felt stupid. She thought about the pretty ceramic pitcher she'd bought for Mrs. Lynch, to thank her for everything she'd done. She had been packing it to make sure it wouldn't be damaged on the trip home and ended up knocking it over. She reacted by trying to catch the pitcher as it broke open against the counter. Chunks of pottery had gashed her palm and thumb.

Tara closed her eyes. There'd been blood everywhere—her clothes, the carpet. She'd grabbed a towel, but she couldn't stop the bleeding. Taking Erin with her, she had no choice but to ask someone from the motel to drive her to the hospital.

"I just want to see my baby," she pleaded.

Finally Erin stopped crying. Tara tried to sit up to see what happened, but she got dizzy. That was when she heard Matt Landers's voice. She opened her eyes and found him standing next to the bed, Erin resting against his broad shoulder.

"Seems this young lady is unhappy," he said.

Although Tara had hated having to call him, she was pleased he was here. "Matt. Thanks for coming."

"Looks like you had a little accident," he said as a pretty blond woman appeared at his side.

Was she Matt's girlfriend? Realizing she was staring, Tara turned away. "It was stupid."

"Well, you did the right thing by coming here."

"Hi, I'm Cari Malone," the woman said. "I'm

married to Dr. Landers's friend Nick. You must be Tara.''

Tara nodded.

''If you let me, I'll hold your little girl until they finish with you.'' Cari leaned forward. ''She looks like she could use a diaper change. And by the sound of her crying, she probably wants a bottle.''

Tara looked at Matt.

''It's okay. Cari was my nurse before she married Nick. She has three kids of her own.'' Matt held Erin away from his shirt to show the wet spot the baby had made.

''I'm sorry,'' Tara said, embarrassed.

''Occupational hazard.'' He gave the baby to Cari, then washed his hands before coming back to Tara to do an examination of his own.

Tara tried to keep focused on Cari changing Erin's diaper, but it was difficult with Matt holding her hand, gently probing her cut.

She was relieved when Dr. Hall returned and took over. ''The laceration is deep. It's going to take some stitches.''

Matt leaned closer. Tara had never had this much attention in her life. ''Think Myers should look at it?''

''I don't have a problem with that,'' the other doctor said.

''What?'' Tara asked. ''Who's Myers?''

''A plastic surgeon. He'll come down to stitch you up,'' Matt explained.

''Is it that bad?''

''No, but why fool around with a scar?'' he said, touching her shoulder. ''Just relax, it won't take long. Besides, we need to get your blood test back.''

"What blood test?" Tara demanded.

"The man from the motel said you nearly passed out. So the lab is running a few tests."

Fifteen minutes later, Dr. Myers showed up and went to work on her hand while Cari managed to get a bottle for Erin and fed her.

"That's it," the doctor announced, finishing the bandage. Then the nurse helped Tara put her arm in a sling. "Don't try to use your hand for about a week. Then I want to see you in my office at the end of the week."

"But I have a baby to care for."

"You don't want to tear the stitches. Surely there's someone who can help you?"

"No—"

"Yes," Matt interrupted as he came into the cubicle, holding her chart. He turned to Dr. Myers. "Tara is a friend of the family. I'll help her find someone to watch the baby."

Tara waited until the doctor left the area. "That won't be necessary," she whispered. "I'm perfectly capable of taking care of Erin."

"Knowing you, you probably could," Matt said. "You're Superwoman. But I just got the result of your blood test. You're anemic, Tara. That's why you got light-headed. Working and taking care of a new baby isn't easy. But don't worry, it's easily corrected with better eating habits and iron pills." He smiled, and she felt a warm tingling in her spine. "I guess this changes your plans," he said.

"How's that?"

"Looks like you won't be going back to Phoenix for a while."

\* \* \*

It was after five o'clock when Matt pulled his car into the driveway of his house with Tara sitting next to him and Erin strapped securely in the carrier in the back seat.

She'd gotten herself in a mess this time, Tara thought.

Matt shut off the engine and climbed out, then hurried around and opened the passenger door. Tara allowed him to help her out of the car. She adjusted her sling to protect her hand as the ocean breeze whipped her hair from her face, teasing her lips with its salty taste.

Had she made a mistake coming here? Tara wondered. Even though she knew Dr. Landers wasn't Erin's father, he was still a stranger. And just a few hours ago, she had agreed to stay at his house. Correction—she agreed to stay in the guest cottage. But she hadn't had much choice, not with twelve stitches in her hand. She was more or less temporarily stuck in Santa Cruz, injured, and she couldn't take care of a baby by herself.

Tara didn't like handouts. She'd had to take them all through her childhood. She and Bri had always been the poor McNeal kids. It had taken years, but Tara had worked hard to stand on her own and banish the pitying looks. She had no choice. Erin was what mattered. She had to accept help again.

Matt opened the back door, unbuckled Erin's baby seat, raised the handle and lifted the carrier from the car. "Come on, little Ms. Erin. Let's go have a look at your new accommodations." Matt started up the walk, then turned and waited for Tara.

She followed, but before she reached the porch,

the door swung open, and Dr. Landers's house-keeper, Juanita, rushed out to greet her.

"Oh, I'm so glad you're here." The older woman glanced at the baby. "And to have a *niña* in the house. Come in."

Tara stepped into the cool, terra-cotta tiled entry. "We're only staying a short time—and in the cottage," she said. "Just until I have my stitches out and can handle the drive back to Phoenix."

"And until then we'll help you with the *niña*." Juanita smiled. "And that will give you plenty of time for a nice vacation. Come inside, I have dinner ready. Then we'll get you and Erin settled."

They walked into the bright kitchen, and Matt set the carrier on the table. Tara pushed the blanket away from Erin and watched as the infant's hands and feet pedaled in the air. Her dark-eyed gaze took in her new surroundings. Tara smiled and touched the baby's soft cheek. Sometimes she couldn't believe that this was her child to raise, to love.

"Do you need to feed the baby?" the housekeeper asked.

"No, Cari Malone fed her," Tara said. "She'll be fine for a while, and with luck she'll fall asleep while I get us moved into the cottage."

"You sit down for awhile," the housekeeper ordered. "Dr. Matt can carry your things from the car. You need to eat."

Tara started to open her month, but Juanita had turned away.

"Don't waste your time arguing," Matt said as he leaned toward her. "You'll only lose."

Tara's breath stopped as she caught a whiff of his

subtle scent. His golden blond hair was slightly mussed, and his mouth curved in a mischievous grin.

Then he turned and walked toward the door. She couldn't help watching his broad shoulders move under a light blue dress shirt that was tucked into his trim waist. His cocoa-brown slacks did nothing to hide his great-looking rear end. Finally he disappeared, and she heard the front door close behind him. *Oh, my. Maybe staying here isn't such a good idea.*

"Come and sit down." The housekeeper came to the table carrying a basket of rolls. "I hope salad and grilled chicken is enough."

Tara jerked her attention to Juanita. "It's perfect. I don't fix much for…just myself." She grabbed Erin's hand and squeezed it. "And with this one I stay so busy, sometimes I can't find a lot of time to eat."

"Oh, I know." The small woman hurried around the kitchen, then came to the table with three Caesar salads. "I raised two sons and a daughter. I couldn't take my eyes off them for a second." She sighed as she glanced at Erin. "They're all grown and married now with children of their own."

"Do they live close by?" Tara asked.

"Michael and Edward are in San Francisco and Elena is in Los Angeles. But I get to visit. After their father died, they wanted me to come live with them." She shook her head. "But I couldn't be a burden to my children. That's when I answered Dr. Matt's ad for a housekeeper. He doesn't really need me to live in, but he knew I'd be alone if I didn't." Another sweet smile touched her lips. "He's a good man."

"No, a smart man…who appreciates a house-keeper who will feed a person at all hours of the day and night."

They both swung around to find Matt had returned. He put the large suitcase and duffel bag in the corner.

"Sit down and eat," ordered Juanita. "Are you going back to the hospital?"

"Yes." He should be leaving now, Matt thought, but he wanted to make sure that Tara was truly staying. He didn't want her taking off. No matter that she shouldn't drive, she might find a way. Even if he had checked her out of the motel and brought all of her things to the cottage. "I thought I'd help get Tara and Erin settled in, then go back and check on a patient in ICU."

He looked at the pretty woman at the table, and their eyes locked.

"There's not much to put away." She nodded to the luggage. "We only have what's there."

"Oh, you have more for the baby now," Juanita announced as she set two plates with grilled chicken and vegetables on the table. "Mr. and Mrs. Malone stopped by when I was cleaning up the cottage. They dropped off a crib and some things for the baby." A big smile appeared on the housekeeper's face as she turned to her boss. "I invited them to come by later. I hope that's okay."

"I always enjoy Nick and Cari's company," Matt said. Even though his entire life had been turned up-side down by the events of the past year, especially the past three days, Matt found himself smiling. He glanced at the baby in the carrier making soft cooing noises, and something stirred in his chest. Then he looked at the slender woman with the short auburn hair and the big, haunting green eyes. The stirring settled lower, and he quickly dropped into the chair next to his new tenant. He had to force himself to think about something else.

"Cari will want to see for herself that you're settled in," he said.

"There's no need," Tara said. She looked a little panicked. "I don't want to intrude on your life."

She already had, from the moment she walked into his office.

"Nick and Cari are good friends," Matt said. "I've also told them about…the situation." He took a bite of salad and after swallowing said, "She just wants to help." Matt stabbed at a piece of chicken, knowing his quiet life was never going to be the same. Why didn't he mind?

Tara's gaze lingered on his face. "I thought you said you didn't want anyone to know." She sent a nervous glance to Juanita.

"That's true. But Juanita and the Malones are close friends, and I trust them. They'll never betray a confidence. Besides, what's to know? Nothing. You're staying in my cottage, not my house."

Her face suddenly reddened as her gaze darted away.

Juanita touched him on the shoulder. "I think Tara is tired. It's been a long day."

Matt sighed. "Right. I'm sorry, Tara. Why don't you eat so we can get you moved into the cottage."

She nodded. "I want to thank you for your help. I don't know what I would have done if you hadn't taken us in. I'm going to repay you…somehow."

Matt wasn't used to seeing this side of Tara McNeal. Something told him that gratitude was hard for her. "I think you're forgetting I need your help, too," he offered.

Tara started to speak, stopped, then began again. "I'm not sure if I want to find the man who…"

Matt raised his hand. "Whoever Erin's father is, you need to find him. Not only because of the promise you made, but to help stop him. He's not ideal father material, but just because you have custody of your niece doesn't mean years later he can't show up and claim her." That was something as a child he had always wished for. He loved his adoptive parents, but there was a hole he'd hoped to fill.

"He could do that?" she asked.

Matt shrugged. "I'm not sure, but it doesn't hurt to be prepared. I could talk with my lawyer."

He watched her back stiffen. "Thank you for the offer, but I can do it when I get home."

"Fine." Why should he care? She could handle her legal affairs. And he needed to concentrate on his business, his life.

The first thing he had to do was find a way to stop reacting to her whenever she got within ten feet of him.

After dinner Matt carried her things to the cottage. Whether Tara liked it or not, the man was going to help her, at least until her hand healed and she could drive home. Juanita eagerly offered to watch Erin while Tara unpacked.

Tara crossed the yard to the cottage porch. She let herself inside to find the quaint little place sparkling, from its windows to the freshly polished floors. Wicker furniture with floral cushions sat in front of a fireplace. Across the room in an alcove a new comforter adorned the bed, and in the corner was a Jenny Lynn crib with soft pink blankets stacked at one end.

"This is lovely," she gasped.

Matt hauled in her few belongings, passed her and set them in the alcove. "Looks like the cleaning fairies have been here."

"I hate that Juanita had to go to so much trouble." Tara was already mesmerized by the wonderful view from the row of windows that overlooked the cliff down to the beach.

"It really wasn't any trouble. And Juanita is crazy about the idea of taking care of a baby."

"But I'm going to pay you."

He shook his head. "You answered enough questions to pay for staying here for a few weeks."

"This view alone is worth a lot."

He glanced at the Pacific Ocean. "It is pretty spectacular." They stood there listening to the surf pounding along the shore.

Tara needed some control. She couldn't let Matt Landers take over. "I can't stay here without paying you something."

She braced herself for an argument, but he didn't say anything. "Whatever you think is fair," he said.

"Well, I can't afford much, but I'd like to give you a hundred dollars a week. I know it doesn't come close to what rent goes for around here, but at least it will feel like I'm contributing."

"Fine. Just make your check out to Juanita Valdez."

"That's it, no argument?"

He tossed her the most endearing grin. "Would it do me any good?"

Tara shook her head.

Matt started to laugh. "Good, then we're both saving a lot of energy." He leaned toward her. "All I want is for us to solve this mystery."

She found herself smiling, too. "And I'll do whatever I can to help."

He nodded, then said, "Later on in the evening, I usually take a walk on the beach. You could come along."

Tara blinked, then quickly shook her head. "I can't leave Erin."

"I believe Cari brought over a baby monitor." He pointed to the crib, and on the table there was a pair of white speakers. "One can go to the house, and if Erin's asleep Juanita can listen for her." He frowned. "Are you sure you don't want to stay in the house? I'd feel better if you were closer."

The deep sound of his seductive voice reverberated through her, causing sensations she didn't want to assess. No way. She couldn't let this man get any closer. Tara shook her head. "We've upset your life enough. Now that Erin is sleeping through the night, I can manage. I'll call if I need any help."

"Well, if you can handle things, I'll head back to the hospital." He carried the suitcase to the bed and opened it. "Call Juanita if you need anything, diapers, formula…"

"Thanks, I will." She gestured with her arm and groaned.

"Are you in pain?" he asked. "I could get you something."

"No, it's not bad."

"Well, just make sure you take your vitamins. And lie down awhile. Juanita is watching the baby."

"I know, but Erin is my responsibility."

He eyed her closely. "You really have a tough time accepting help."

"I like to pay my own way."

He smiled again, and her heart tripped. "I'll see what I can find for a one-armed woman to do." He turned serious. "Tara, I appreciate your talking with Jim. I know it wasn't easy."

"No, it wasn't," was all she said.

They stood there for what seemed like an eternity, his brown eyes so intent on her face that shivers ran down her spine. Finally she managed to tear her gaze away. "I guess I've kept you long enough."

He checked his watch. "I do need to get back. I'll see you later. Take your time unpacking. Believe me, Juanita doesn't mind in the least watching Erin." He started for the door, and Tara followed. He suddenly stopped and turned. Unable to prevent it, she ran into the solid wall of his chest. He reached out and grabbed her by the upper arms to steady her.

"You okay?" he asked. "Did I hurt you—your hand?"

"No, I'm fine." The pressure of his hands on her arms was firm, warm.

He released her. "I just wanted to tell you the phone works and there's also an intercom button to the house. Just in case you need anything."

*I need you to leave so I can breathe again,* she thought. "Thank you."

"Then I'll see you later."

He turned and left.

Tara fell against the closed door and drew a deep breath into her starved lungs. She had to stop looking at the man as if he was a sinfully delicious fudge sundae. He was just a man. Yeah, right. And what she needed to remember was the trouble her sister had gotten into because she trusted a man. A good-looking sweet-talking man.

She knew that the Matt Landers she'd met and gotten to know in the past few days wasn't the man who ran out on her sister. In fact Dr. Landers seemed nothing short of a nice guy. But something about him raised a red flag. His charm. His ready smile. Or was it the way he drew everyone's attention, especially women? There was no doubt he was a successful doctor and had the respect of the community.

Tara remembered another man who could charm everyone, had the same good looks. Sean McNeal. He had been a nice guy, too. Still, he could disappear faster than Houdini. He could make convincing promises, then be gone the next day, taking any money his wife had managed to save.

Tara had tried to understand why her father always left them. Why his family hadn't been enough to keep him home. Then after a while she had just stopped waiting for him to come back. Over the years, she'd built a wall around herself, not letting anyone get too close, except for her mother and Bri.

Now she had Erin. Erin was her family. And Tara was going to do everything she could to protect both herself and her niece from anyone who might hurt them, including Matt Landers.

Matt made a quick trip into his study and called the Malone house. When Cari answered, he asked if she and Nick could postpone their visit until tomorrow night, and if Cari would stop by in the morning to check on Tara. She readily accepted.

Matt thanked her, then said goodbye and hung up. He drew a breath, thinking about his two female houseguests. He knew his quiet, sedate life was about to change.

He walked into the kitchen to say goodbye to Juanita, who was busy washing the dishes.

"The Malones aren't coming tonight. Tara needs to rest."

Juanita looked up and smiled. "I'll make sure she does."

"Thanks," he said, knowing that Juanita would more than take care of Tara and the baby. "I know it's short notice but I invited Cari and Nick to dinner tomorrow."

That awarded him another smile from the housekeeper as she put a pot in the sink and began scrubbing it. "I'm glad to see you're going to entertain some friends. You work too hard."

He watched her for a moment, knowing no matter what he said, she wouldn't be convinced. "I'm a doctor, Juanita. I can't help it if I'm needed. Besides, I have surgery scheduled tomorrow morning. I need to check on my patient tonight."

"I'm not talking about you being a surgeon. I'm talking about all those fancy cocktail parties and dinners you go to."

He smiled. "I thought you wanted me to go out."

"I want you to out for *fun*. Find someone to spend time with, not be a puppet for that…hotshot Harry Douglas."

No matter how many times Matt told his housekeeper that he'd probably never marry and have a family, she continued to encourage him to find that special someone.

"What I do brings donations to the hospital for research. It helps those children who can't afford the treatment they need."

"I know, I know," she chanted. "But wouldn't you like to come home and find someone waiting for you?"

Matt blocked out the dream as he wrapped his arms around the diminutive woman. "I do. You greet me with a smile every night." He kissed her cheek.

She giggled before she pushed him away. "You are *loco*. Go back to work so I can."

He started to leave when she stopped him.

"Wait, Dr. Matt. Before you leave will you check on the baby?" She raised her soapy hands. "Little Erin is in the guest room."

Matt went down the hall to the first doorway past his den. The room had been painted a soft blue and had plush carpeting. The double bed against the wall had a mahogany carved headboard that had belonged to his parents, and his mother's parents before that. The white satin comforter had been pulled back to the foot of the bed, and a circle of pillows surrounded the precious bundle in the middle.

He stepped into the room, deciding to keep his distance. He glanced at the sleeping baby dressed in a pink stretch suit. Her tiny fist was against her mouth, and she was making sucking noises in her sleep. A familiar longing tightened his chest. Closing his eyes, he hoped to block out the scene, making resisting easier. It didn't work.

Finally, he walked to the bed and sat on the edge. He drew a deep breath, and the soft scent of baby powder filled his nostrils. He watched the sleeping infant take a slumbering breath. Reaching out his hand, he gently stroked her head.

''Looks like you and I are going to spend some time together,'' he whispered.

Slowly a pair of big brown eyes opened wide and stared at him. Matt froze as Erin's sleepy gaze moved over his face, as if memorizing this new stranger in her life. Then surprisingly she reached out and trustingly gripped his finger.

That was the moment Matt lost his heart.

## Chapter Five

Tara was awakened the next morning by Erin's soft cry. She rolled over and groaned, feeling the soreness in her injured hand.

No sooner had she gotten out of bed than Juanita appeared at the door. Dressed in a bright turquoise blouse and dark slacks, the housekeeper held up a plate of food and a baby bottle.

Tara got up and managed to unlatch the door and let her in.

"I heard on the baby monitor that our girl was awake," Juanita said as she swept into the room. "I have both your breakfasts ready." The woman dropped off a plate on the table, then went to the crib and smiled at her new charge. She spoke a few words in Spanish, then picked up the baby. "Let's get you a dry diaper and then we'll have some breakfast." Erin immediately stopped crying as the older woman changed her. Then Juanita carried the freshly diapered baby to the sofa and began to feed her the bottle.

Juanita looked at Tara. "Sit down and eat. Don't forget your vitamins, either."

Tara nodded, went to the table and uncovered a plate of scrambled eggs and bacon. Her stomach grumbled. Last night she'd been too nervous to eat much dinner. But this was a lot more than she ever ate in the morning. "This is so much," she said.

"Dr. Matt thinks you need to put on ten pounds."

Why did the fact that Matt thought she was skinny bother her? Of course, a man built as solid and muscular as the doctor believed in perfection. Probably in his women, too. Well, too bad. Tara had no intention of stuffing herself to satisfy the good doctor.

"How did you sleep?" Juanita asked.

Her question brought Tara back from her reverie. "Not bad. My hand hurt a little. But I managed." She picked up the fork with her good right hand, recalling the trouble she'd had getting to sleep. It hadn't been just the discomfort in her hand.

"Did you take the pills Dr. Matt gave you?"

Tara shook her head, studying her bandaged hand. "No, I didn't want to. Erin might have needed me."

"I understand. But I'm close by. Just let me know when you need to take one, and I'll be happy to watch her." Juanita gazed at the baby in her arms. "She's so precious."

Tara knew she shouldn't be upset that Juanita wanted to help—she should be grateful—but she had planned to spend the summer taking care of Erin herself. Now, thanks to her clumsiness, it looked like she was going to have to delay that idea for a while.

"Juanita, I can't thank you enough for helping me out."

The older woman raised the baby to her shoulder and began gently patting her back. "I love it. Taking care of a baby is a joy."

Tara hated handouts, and here she was living in Matt Landers's house for next to nothing, and his housekeeper was Erin's baby-sitter.

There was another knock at the door. "Hello, is anyone home?" Cari Malone peeked inside the cottage and smiled. "Good morning. I hope you don't mind, but when no one came to the door, I walked around back."

The petite blonde was dressed in a red and blue print skirt with a denim vest covering an eggshell T-shirt. On her feet were white leather Keds. She wore her thick hair pinned high on her head.

"No, please come in," Tara said as she stood. She brushed her messy hair from her face, then tried to close her worn bathrobe, but couldn't quite manage with one hand.

"Please, finish eating," Cari said. "I thought I'd stop by and see if there's anything you need. I volunteer at the hospital this morning and was wondering, Tara, if you'd like to get out of the house for a few hours and come with me."

"You want me to volunteer?"

Cari smiled. "Sure, if you want. I'm pulling duty in the day-care center. And since you're a teacher, I bet you could handle reading a few stories, even with one hand."

"But I have Erin to take care of."

"I'll watch her," Juanita offered. "She'll go down

for a nap, anyway. She'll be sleeping most of the time you're gone."

"And we can stop by the store and get some things you need for both you and the baby," Cari added. "Personal things you might not want a man to buy you."

"I do need to make arrangements about my car. I'd like to stop by the motel and thank the manager for bringing me to the hospital."

"Good, I'll drive you," Cari said. "Now, go get ready. If you want, I'll wrap your hand in plastic so you can shower."

"Thanks, that would be great." Tara smiled. She liked Cari Malone. She had been a big help yesterday after the accident, and Tara was excited about spending the morning with her.

It took another thirty minutes before Tara was presentable. She wore the same navy slacks she had on last night, but added a pink T-shirt and strappy brown sandals. She kissed Erin goodbye, then followed Cari to her late model minivan, and soon they were on their way to the hospital. Tara found herself wondering if she'd get to see Matt.

Once they arrived at the hospital, they went to the day-care center on the ground floor. It was impressive, to say the least.

Cari explained to Tara how hard it had been to get the project off the ground, especially when the hospital administrator felt the center was a waste of money. The last three years had been like a war, fighting to get what Riverhaven employees needed so badly. But in the end, and thanks to some more of the Malone money, the day-care center had become a reality.

Tara was introduced to the director, then shown around the facility. The spacious rooms included a nursery outfitted with several cribs and a classroom for the older kids who used the center when school was out. The children ranged from infants to five years old, and parents could come and visit during their lunch hour.

Charlene, the director, assigned Tara to the four- and five-year-olds. She read to them, even managed to get the kids organized to draw some pictures. With all the busy activity, the morning disappeared before Tara realized it, and the children were led away to the lunchroom.

Cari appeared with Charlene, a plump thirty-something woman with brown hair pulled into a loose bun. "I can't thank you enough for coming in to help," the director said. "We're really short-handed right now."

"I had a good time." Tara raised her bandaged hand. "I wish I could have done more."

"Well, you did fine. If you ever want a job, just let me know."

"Thank you for the offer, but I'm only visiting. I'll be going back to Phoenix soon."

"I knew you were too good to be true. Thanks again." The director sighed and walked away.

"My, my," Cari began. "I've never heard that woman so complimentary."

"All I did was read a few stories and draw some pictures."

"I know for a fact it had to be more than that.

The older kids are always a little hard to handle. They don't like to be in school in the summertime."

"Maybe the center should think about taking field trips one day a week during summer months. Help the kids burn off some energy."

"Great idea. I'll run it past Charlene. Let me grab my purse. I'll be right back."

Tara was putting away the books and straightening the miniature chairs when she glanced up and saw Matt in the doorway watching her. She put the last book away, then went to him. He looked tired. Even when he smiled, she could see the fatigue etched around his eyes. He even looked good in green scrubs, she decided.

"Good morning," he said.

She raised an eyebrow. "It's almost noon."

He smiled again. "Not quite, so it's still morning."

She nodded, finding it difficult to breathe.

"How was your night?" he asked.

"Not bad. And yours? Looks like you've already been in surgery."

"Yeah, at seven this morning."

"How did it go?"

"The patient's condition is guarded." He sighed. "I just spent an hour in recovery. Then the nurse threw me out."

"I'm sure everything is going to be fine." Time lapsed as they stood there in silence.

"How did you know I was here?" she asked.

"I called home and Juanita told me." He glanced at her bandaged hand. "I take it your stitches aren't bothering you today."

"Not much." She brushed her hair from her face

and bit on her lower lip, realizing she hadn't been able to put on any makeup this morning.

"Well, how do you like our center?" he asked.

"It's...great. My kindergarten class back in Phoenix didn't have as much."

His dark gaze moved over her face. "Riverhaven has a lot to offer."

Like one of the country's best heart surgeons, she thought silently. She decided it best to change the subject. "I want to concentrate on Erin." She held up her wounded hand. "But it looks like I can't even do that."

Matt watched Tara's disappointment take the light from her eyes. "Give your hand a week to heal," he said, "then you can take over caring for your niece again."

She looked at him, her green eyes shimmering. "I know, but I feel so helpless," she said in a breathy voice.

Unable to move, Matt could only stare at her. Tara was a beautiful woman, and not just her face, but her heart. He'd watched her with the kids earlier, saw her natural patience and caring, which could only come from a big heart. That made Tara McNeal the most dangerous kind of woman for him to become attracted to...the kind of woman who was meant to have a home, a family. The kind he should walk away from. But this time it was going to be more difficult than in the past.

The spell was broken by a familiar voice. "There you two are."

Matt jerked his head around to see Cari walking toward them.

"Time for lunch," she said, smiling. "Ready to join two good-looking ladies for a bite to eat?"

"Maybe I should get home," Tara said.

Cari shook her head. "Come on, you earned a break. You worked hard this morning." Cari turned to Matt. "Charlene even offered Tara a job."

He smiled. "Then we should celebrate at lunch." When Tara started to object, he added, "I have only a little time, though."

All three rode the elevator down to the first floor and made their way to the cafeteria. The room was already busy with the lunch crowd. Cari and Matt volunteered to get the food while Tara searched for a place to sit.

After finding a table, Tara looked at the doctors and nurses buzzing around her. What a difference a week made. She was in a strange town, living in a stranger's house. She glanced at her hand. And by the looks of it, she was staying awhile.

Tara had never been a wanderer like her sister. She was content staying close to home. She knew she didn't need to worry about her house in Phoenix. Mrs. Lynch would watch things for her. It was just this displaced feeling she had, and the fact she'd allowed a virtual stranger to take over her life.

A shiver rippled through Tara as she looked across the room and watched Matt in line. He towered over the other men, and it wasn't just his height. It was his presence, the way he carried himself, the way he smiled…. She glanced away. She had to stop thinking about him as a man. Well, he was a man, of course. But not Erin's father.

A few minutes later, Cari and Matt arrived at the table.

"Hope you like ham and cheese," Cari said.

"It's fine."

The food was unloaded, and Matt returned both trays to the counter. On his way back, Tara watched him greet people with an easy smile and an air of confidence. He was the renowned Dr. Landers, and she'd never felt so out of place.

Matt took the seat next to her. "Well, how are you holding up after spending the morning with a bunch of kids?"

"Nothing to it. Remember I teach kindergartners."

Cari caught Tara's attention. "Too bad you're not staying in the area. We could use you at the center." She turned to Matt. "Oh, by the way, I told Charlene that Tara is a friend of mine and that she and her daughter are staying part of the summer."

Matt shrugged. "There isn't any reason she should know more."

"If there's a problem," Tara began.

"There isn't a problem with you staying," Matt said. "Remember you're helping me. Besides, you can't drive back to Phoenix with those sutures in your hand."

"I see the doctor at the end of the week. I'll be out of your hair soon."

"You're not a problem," he said.

Tara couldn't help but stare at Matt. His handsome face was tan, and his hair had been streaked by the sun. His lashes and brows were darker, making his brown eyes stand out. His mouth had tiny laugh lines at the corners. Her gaze drifted to his lips, and she wondered about the feel and the taste of him. Suddenly she felt her face flush, with good reason. She had to get control of her thoughts.

"You need someone getting in your hair," Cari murmured, and Matt glared at her. Then he turned to Tara.

"You're not eating," he said. "Is your sandwich okay?"

"Oh, it's fine." She picked up her ham and cheese and took a bite.

Matt steered the conversation to another topic but had trouble concentrating on what Cari was talking about. Tara was too close. She made it impossible for him to think about anything else. He recalled his crazy move the other night when he nearly kissed her. Stay away from her, he told himself...again.

"Dr. Landers."

Matt recognized the voice and wished he could ignore it. Instead he glanced up and saw the hospital administrator, Harry Douglas, approaching the table. The white-haired man in his mid-sixties was unsmiling.

"Harry," Matt said.

Harry turned to the women seated at the table. "Hello, Cari."

"Hello, Harry."

He focused on Tara. "I don't believe we've met."

Cari did the honors. "Harry, this is a friend of mine, Tara McNeal. Tara, this is Harry Douglas."

He extended his hand. "Nice to meet you, Ms. McNeal."

Tara shook it. "Thank you, Mr. Douglas."

Harry released her hand and looked at Matt. "Dr. Landers, do you think I could see you for a minute...in private?"

Matt stood and followed the man out of the cafeteria. He had nothing against Harry. At least he hadn't until his wallet had been stolen and the creditors began calling the hospital wanting financial restitution from their top surgeon. Since then the administrator had been dogging Matt's every step.

"What can I do for you, Harry?"

"I hear that the Gentry kid isn't doing well. I told you, Matt, he wasn't a good candidate for the surgery."

"Look, Harry, Ryan is doing as well as can be expected considering his condition had been ignored for so long." Matt tried not to hold a grudge against this man, but if Harry had his way, some of the less fortunate kids wouldn't be able to get the benefits of Riverhaven Hospital. "And I'm keeping a close eye on him," Matt added.

"Be sure that you do," the administrator warned. "It wouldn't be good for the hospital if we lost this patient, especially since we've gotten so much publicity because of his case." He gave Matt the once-over. "Let's hope you live up to your reputation, Doctor." How soon Harry had forgotten how much acclaim and donations Matt had brought to the hospital. "Speaking of publicity, have you gotten that credit-card mess straightened out?"

Matt managed to control his anger, but just barely. "I'm handling it."

"Make sure you do. With the charity ball coming up we don't need any negative press."

Before Matt could say anything, Harry turned and marched off. Why did he put up with this? Matt thought. There were plenty of other hospitals that would be happy to have him on staff. But he knew he would run into the same problems. Most hospitals nowadays were concerned about costs and making money. Riverhaven relied heavily on research grants and wealthy donors. Thanks to both, the hospital was one of the top cardiac facilities in the country.

And truth be known, Matt didn't want to be anywhere else. But that didn't stop him from wanting to tell Harry that he didn't give a flying leap about the cost of lifesaving surgery. Every patient deserved the best care, whether he had the money for it or not.

His pager went off, and he glanced at the message. It was recovery. The six-year-old boy needed him. Matt headed to the elevators, then passed them up for the stairs. He was going to do everything he could to help the young patient survive and live a normal life. Every child deserved that.

Tara watched Matt walk away. He wasn't coming back to lunch.

"Looks like the good Dr. Landers isn't going to be able to finish his meal." Cari sighed. "I wish he'd take better care of himself. Sleeping at the hospital and not eating isn't good for him." The petite woman started to laugh. "I'm sounding like a mother."

"You care about him," Tara said.

"Yeah, I care. Matt's a good friend. Damn the man who's trying to ruin him." She shook her head. "In all the years I've known Matt, he's been very discreet, kept his life private. Going off and having a vacation fling isn't…" She shook her head. "It's not Matt. He may tease and act friendly with people around the hospital, but he's always the professional.

He's never even dated anyone who works here at Riverhaven.''

Tara could see how upset Cari was. "I came to Santa Cruz because my sister asked me to. But I know now that Matt is as much a victim as Bri and Erin.''

Cari touched Tara's hand as she smiled. "I hope you get to know Matt like I do. He doesn't deserve any of this mess.''

Tara was learning more about Matt Landers than she needed to know.

"When I was hired here five years ago,'' Cari began, "it was Matt who made me feel welcome.'' She got a dreamy look in her eyes. "Who would have thought that Nick and I would get together?''

Tara found she was envious. She'd never had a long-lasting relationship, never made the time for dating. Now, as much as she wanted a family for Erin, it was going to be difficult for her to find someone willing to love her and her child.

"It's funny how things change,'' Cari continued. "Not that it was easy to get together. We had to tackle a lot of obstacles. Matt was a big help. He's always been a good friend to both of us. Helped me through some rough times after my daughter died.''

Tara's heart jumped into her throat. "Oh, Cari, I had no idea.''

Cari leaned back in her chair and remained silent for a moment. "Not many people do. My first husband and daughter died in an automobile accident over six years ago. Angela. We called her Angel. She was only two years old.''

Tara knew how hard it was to lose her sister, but a child...

"It's been a long time, but you never forget." Cari drew a long breath. "It's funny how your life unfolds. I'm originally from Washington State, and after Angel died, I needed closure. I came to Riverhaven to begin again. That's how I met Danny and Nick. Danny and I were crazy about each other from the start. But Nick didn't like me very much. He didn't like many women back then. His first wife had left him when Danny was fighting for his life and needed a heart transplant. So trust wasn't a word in his vocabulary when it came to women.

"I became Danny's nurse, and I ended up moving into the Malone home." She smiled. "Nick and I eventually fell in love, but it wasn't an easy road. I don't believe real love ever is.

"During the rough times, Matt helped me. He set me up with a support group. He's a wonderful man. He's the godfather to our little Matthew."

Tara and Cari exchanged a long look, then Cari spoke again. "Erin would be one lucky little girl if Matt were her father."

That evening at Matt's home, Tara could hear the voices and laughter all the way back to the guest bedroom where she finally managed to get Erin's sleeper on using one hand.

She surveyed her work, then stood and checked her navy pleated slacks and pink cotton sweater in the mirror.

"Not bad." Of course not much went with a pale-gray cotton sling. It had been her sister, Bri, who'd been able to walk into a room and wow everyone. Tara had been the shy sister who didn't take to strangers. But Cari wasn't a stranger after their day spent together, not after all the things Cari had told her about her past and starting over in Santa Cruz.

Tara watched her niece contentedly sucking on her fist. The child had no idea what was going on, and that was the way Tara wanted it. She hoped Erin would never know about any of this. She straightened the cute white elastic bow on the child's head. "You're just going to charm 'em, sweetie," she whispered.

Matt appeared at the bedroom door.

"Tara."

"Oh, Matt," she said. Her gaze wandered over his casual clothes. Tonight he wore a pair of fitted jeans and a blue open-collared shirt that gave him a whole new appeal. She looked at his face. Big mistake. His deep brown eyes were compelling, almost magnetic.

He finally broke the spell when he spoke. "You ready?"

"Sure. If you would put Erin in the carrier for me," she said.

"My pleasure." He smiled as he approached the bed and reached past her for the carrier. That was when she caught a whiff of his soap and soft musk aftershave.

"Come on, Miss Erin," he said.

Erin waved her arms and smiled as he lifted her expertly into the carrier. Then Matt escorted them both into the den.

Tara's attention focused on the couple seated on the sofa. Cari, dressed in jeans and a sweater, sat next to a handsome black-haired man dressed in the same casual way.

Smiling, Cari stood and came up to her. "Hi, Tara.

Long time no see.'' She turned to the man beside her. "This is my husband, Nick."

Nick Malone was a little taller than Matt, but their builds were nearly the same. Nick was as dark as Matt was blond. He had gray eyes that were more curious than friendly. No doubt he felt protective of his friend.

"Hello, Tara." He reached out and shook her good hand, then finally offered her a guarded smile. "Heard you had an accident."

"I wasn't paying attention to what I was doing." She grimaced as she held up her hand.

Cari glanced at Erin and smiled. "Oh, she looks adorable," she said, gushing. "May I hold her?"

When Tara nodded, Cari took the carrier and set it on the desk, then lifted the baby in her arms.

The sound of Cari's baby talk and Erin's cooing filled the room. Finally Nick smiled. "As you can see, my wife is crazy about kids. We have three of our own." He glanced over his shoulder at his wife as Matt appeared at Tara's side, surprising her by resting his hand against her lower back.

"Would you like a drink before dinner?" he asked.

"No, thank you." She moved away from his touch and walked to the sofa where Cari was playing with Erin.

"She's very alert for three months," the blonde said. "And so happy." Just then Erin gave them all a big toothless grin as her arms and legs pumped the air.

Both Cari and Tara laughed.

Tara looked up and discovered Matt's gaze on her.

His dark eyes held hers, and a rush of heat surged
through her.

"This is such a cute age," Cari said. "Taking care
of a baby can be tiring, but at this stage they sleep
a lot."

Tara forced her attention to Cari. "Erin is fascinated with the mobile in the crib. Thank you for letting her use it."

"You're welcome. Our third child, Matthew, is
nearly a year old, so we have plenty of baby things
around." Cari's gaze went to her husband, and they
shared a private look. "They're not being used right
now."

Tara couldn't miss the loving exchange between
the couple. She glanced at Matt, knowing he'd seen
it, too. "I'll take good care of all your things. We
won't be staying too long," Tara said.

"You *are* staying until the stitches come out,"
Matt insisted, then looked at Cari. "I've been hoping
Tara will join forces with Jim and me to find this
imposter."

"I don't know what else I can help you with,"
Tara said, knowing that she didn't fit in here. This
wasn't a life-style she was used to. And now that she
knew Matt wasn't Erin's father, her niece didn't be-
long here, either.

Cari cradled Erin closer. "I meant to tell you earlier, I'm so sorry about your sister. Your niece is
lucky to have you."

Tara sighed. "Thank you."

"It's such a shame that this mess had to happen,"
Cari said, then her voice grew wistful. "Who
wouldn't want this beautiful child?"

Matt watched Tara, not wanting to even think

about Cari's question. From personal experience he knew that not everyone wanted a baby. Not everyone craved a child like he did. He'd already begun to care for little Erin…and for Tara. He glanced away. Damn. Stop thinking about her. He had to put all his energy into finding the man who was trying to destroy his life.

They all turned in Juanita's direction when she walked in and announced that dinner was ready. Matt picked up the carrier and escorted Tara. Nick put his arm around his wife as they all went into the dining room, where Juanita had laid out a Mexican feast.

"Great, all my favorites," Nick said as he hugged the older woman. "Thank you, Juanita. You make the best Mexican food around."

The housekeeper smiled. "You're welcome. Now sit down and eat before the food gets cold."

Nick and Cari took their seats across the table, and Matt pulled out the chair next to his for Tara. Juanita appeared at her side and took the carrier. "I'll take the little *niña.*"

"But you don't have to," Tara said.

"You enjoy your meal. This little one and I are becoming good friends."

Matt saw Tara's worried look as the two left the room. "Juanita loves being with Erin."

"I know, I'm being silly." Embarrassed, she glanced around the table. "But Erin has met so many strangers in the last few days. In Phoenix, the only other person she was with was my neighbor who watched her while I finished out the school year." And now, with her arm in a sling, Tara couldn't even hold her. She missed the feel of Erin's warm little body in her arms.

"Well, she seems to thrive on the attention," Cari said. "And if you're worried about Erin not thinking of you as her...mother, well, she does. All the time I was holding her, whenever she heard your voice, she turned in your direction."

Tara smiled. "I'm new at this...motherhood stuff. I'm never sure of my instincts when it comes to Erin's care."

"You're doing just fine," Cari assured her. "And it's natural for you to feel that way. I have to warn you, Tara, the fear doesn't ever go away." She grabbed her husband's hand. "We all have a tendency to be overprotective, but kids need to be nurtured and loved, not isolated."

"She's talking about me," Nick said. "I'm...cautious when it comes to our kids."

Matt grinned as he dished up cheese enchiladas and handed Tara a filled plate. "That's putting it mildly."

"Hey, just you wait, Doc. Someday, hopefully soon, you'll know what I'm talking about from first-hand experience."

A pain shot straight to Matt's heart, but he managed to keep a pleasant smile on his face. No one, not even his best friend, knew that for him, having a family was an impossible dream.

At nine o'clock, Matt waved goodbye to the Malones as they pulled out of the driveway. It had been a nice evening. With a yawn, he returned to the house to find Tara holding the carrier with Erin.

"I'll say good-night, too," she said, and headed for the patio door.

"I'll walk you to the cottage." He stared at the

pretty redhead in the pale pink sweater and wanted more time with her. "Make sure you're both settled in for the night." He didn't want to think about Tara McNeal in bed, either. "It has been a long day."

She nodded. "Thank you for having us to dinner. The Malones are nice."

"The best," he said as he took the carrier from her. They walked out the door and across the yard. He could feel her closeness as they shared the brick pathway to the cottage porch. Even in the cool evening breeze his body was heating up. They made it up the single step to the cottage, and he opened the door.

"Well, thank you again," she said as she tried to go around him.

"Here, let me get—" He reached inside, then without warning she grabbed for the switch and they collided.

Matt bit back a groan as her body brushed against his. The moonlight illuminated the room enough so he could see the outline of her face, and he felt her rapid breathing.

Then her head raised to his, and her eyes widened. Unable to stop himself, he lowered his head. Curiosity and need brought his mouth toward hers. Why had she stirred up these thoughts in his head—needy and hungry thoughts?

That's when his beeper sounded, and Tara jumped back. Matt turned on the light and looked down to read the number on his pager. The hospital.

Quickly he carried the baby to the crib. He set the carrier down, gently lifted Erin out and laid her on her bed. She made a soft whimpering sound, then went back to sleep. He covered her with a blanket.

Matt stepped away. "Juanita has the baby monitor in her room, so if either of you need anything, let her know."

"I will. I hope everything turns out okay at the hospital."

"So do I," he said. He looked once more at Tara. Big mistake. Somehow he managed to back out the door. "Good night."

"Good night," Tara whispered. Once Matt was out of sight, she turned on the overhead light and went to the crib. Erin was sleeping soundly, and Tara touched her rosy cheek.

"Oh, sweetie, I better be careful. There's so much that could happen." She thought of Bri. "And I can't let you get hurt." She stepped away from the crib, then went into the small kitchen area. She opened the refrigerator and pulled out a can of soda.

Things had gotten way out of hand, Tara thought. What had gotten into her? She didn't go around kissing men she hardly knew. Okay, she hadn't kissed him. But she'd wanted to.

She could count on her fingers the number of men she'd kissed in her life. She'd never had much time to date in between working and going to classes. In high school, a skinny, freckled girl was not the boys' first choice.

College hadn't been much different. She met a few guys, but mostly she preferred a comfortable friendship. Never had any man's touch affected her the way Matt Landers's had. She thought about the almost kiss and quickly shook it away.

She needed to think about a man who would be more her type. Who would be suited to her and her quiet life-style. A man who wanted the same things she did, a home and kids. He'd already told her in so many words that his career was his life. Beside, what would a high-powered doctor see in her?

Tara sat on the sofa, but her mind refused to stop thinking of Matt. She had to find a way to stay clear of the man. But that was impossible, now that she was practically living in his house.

She knew that Matt wasn't Erin's father, but deep down, she wished he was. But that was a secret she would always keep to herself.

# Chapter Six

At nine the next morning, Matt rolled his stiff shoulders as the crisp ocean breeze blew through the car window, helping him keep awake. Sleeping off and on last night on his office sofa hadn't been at all restful. But his patient had made it through the crisis. And now Matt was headed home to bed and sleep.

Was that possible? he wondered as he turned off the highway onto the road leading to his house. He found he was looking forward to seeing Tara. How had she and Erin gotten along? The last he'd heard from Juanita, things were going well.

During his all-night vigil at the hospital with his patient, Matt managed to find time to think about the attractive redhead. He tried to tell himself that it was because she was living in the cottage and he'd been the one who'd talked her into staying there. She was his responsibility. But to his chagrin, he realized that what he was thinking about was his overwhelming urge to kiss her. Damn. Nearly giving in to his desire was definitely a stupid move.

He drove up the driveway and into the open garage. After shutting off the engine, he closed his eyes. Somehow, he had to find a way to keep his distance from the woman. Stick to business, he told himself. He needed Tara McNeal to help with the investigation. That had to be his focus, because the two Ms. McNeals had somehow managed to turn his quiet and once contented life upside down.

Little Erin didn't deserve a father who used people, who lied and stole. A familiar yearning settled in Matt's gut. He couldn't let his desire for this child cloud his common sense. He wasn't Erin's father and never could be.

It wasn't as if he'd never wanted a family. Having been adopted, he'd dreamed of having a blood relative. He had even been engaged once. His first year as a resident he'd met and fallen in love with a beautiful woman, a nurse named Julie Atkins.

From a routine test in med school, he'd discovered his nearly nonexistent sperm count. Julie told him she could handle it, but only months into the engagement, she finally admitted she didn't want a marriage that couldn't produce children.

Over the years, Matt kept his secret, feeling as if he were flawed. His imperfection made him bad husband material. So he picked his dates accordingly, women who were career driven, uninterested in marriage. He never got close enough to worry about commitment or of being shunned. No, love wasn't for him.

Matt climbed out of the car and looked toward the

cottage, thinking of the two pretty females who had invaded his quiet life. He warned himself to be careful. He drew a deep breath, knowing that didn't mean his heart would listen.

Around one o'clock, after sleep and a shower, Matt felt almost human. Once he called the hospital and found that his young patient was still improving, Matt went into the kitchen to find Juanita. His stomach growled when the aroma of soup teased his nose, reminding him that he'd skipped a few meals.

"It's a good thing you have me around to keep meat on those bones," the housekeeper teased. "I'm cooking one of your favorites for dinner. Pot roast."

He smiled. "And gravy?"

She gave him a once-over. "Who'd ever think you were a heart doctor? You know all that fat isn't good for you." She went to the stove and brought a bowl of soup to the table. "Sit and eat."

Matt eagerly did her bidding. "Once or twice a year isn't going to kill me," he informed her. "Besides, I take good care of myself." He patted his flat stomach, remembering he hadn't gone running in over a week.

"Oh, yeah," the housekeeper began, "like the past two days. I bet you didn't get enough sleep and you ate that awful food from the machines." She returned with some rolls and butter.

Matt eagerly started in on the tortilla soup. "If I didn't I wouldn't appreciate your cooking so much."

"You need a wife. She would give you plenty of reason to come home."

"No woman would put up with me."

Juanita gave him a secret look. "The right woman would."

Matt had stopped believing that a long time ago. He'd finished his soup when he heard the baby crying over the monitor.

"There she is. I was wondering if she was going to wake up." Juanita wiped her hands, then pulled a bottle from the microwave. "Why don't you take this down to the cottage and feed Erin? Then convince Tara to come to dinner. She's been hiding out in the cottage all day. Ever since that package came for her."

Was it the address book? Matt wondered. Deciding he was going to find out, he took the bottle. "Has Tara been eating?"

Juanita nodded. "She had breakfast, and I brought over lunch."

"Thanks, Juanita." He hugged her. "You've been a big help."

She pushed him away. "It's about time I had something to do around here. Now go feed that little one. Be careful, she might steal your heart."

Matt smiled. "I have that problem with every kid I see at the hospital." He hurried out of the kitchen, grabbed his medical bag off the desk in his office, then stepped outside and crossed the lawn to the cottage.

So Tara McNeal didn't want to be a bother. Well, it was too late for that. He hadn't been able to get her out of his head for the past week.

Okay, he shouldn't have almost kissed her. But he *hadn't* kissed her. The only question was, how long could he resist? How long could he resist that sweet mouth of hers? Resist teasing her lips into parting and allowing him inside to taste her secrets…

*Whoa, cool your jets, fella. Forget that Tara is the first woman in a long time you've been attracted to. She's off-limits. You need to feed Erin and examine Tara's wound, then get the hell out,* he told himself as he stepped up on the porch and knocked. The door opened and Tara appeared, looking frazzled. Her hair had more curl than he remembered as the bright sunlight caught its reddish highlights. The sun also illuminated the freckles across her nose and cheeks. Even without a lick of makeup, she was beautifully wholesome.

Her green eyes widened. "Matt, what are you doing here?"

He nodded over her shoulder. "By the sound coming from the littlest McNeal, she's hungry. And your hand needs to be checked."

She shook her head. "Really, it's fine."

Stubborn woman. Matt refused to let her dismiss him and stepped inside the cottage. The room was warm and already smelled like her, a mixture of citrus and powder. A shot of desire went through him. He set his bag on the table, then quickly crossed the room to find Erin in the crib, crying, her legs kicking in anger.

"Hey, what's wrong?" She quieted down as he finished with the diapering Tara must have started, then he put Erin's little suit on. He picked her up and placed the bottle to her lips, and immediately the baby drew the nipple into her mouth. Her tiny fingers latched onto Matt's as he carried her to the sofa.

Tara sat across from him. "I managed to get her changed, but I couldn't pick her up."

He looked up and saw Tara's frustration. "I'm glad you didn't. Just be patient. As soon as the stitches are out, you can go back to caring for Erin on your own."

When Tara started to argue, Matt interrupted her. "Look, Tara, you know it will be best for everyone if you just accept it."

"Easy for you to say. It's hard to do when there's a baby who needs you. And I can't have you and Juanita running out here all the time. You have your own lives."

"My life is constantly disrupted," he said. "I'm a doctor. Juanita has a normal routine for the first time in all the years she's worked for me. And you know she loves to care for Erin. Her own grandkids are far away. Are you going to deprive her of the simple pleasures of caring for this child?"

She brushed her hair from her face. "I guess not."

"Good." He smiled as he lifted Erin to his shoulder and began to pat her back. Tara went to get a diaper and laid it against his shirt.

"She's been spitting up a little."

The baby burped, and Matt finished giving her the rest of her bottle. Then he placed her in the carrier and turned his attention to Tara.

"I want to examine your hand."

She started to argue, then relented. "Okay."

They sat at the table. Tara pulled her arm out of the sling, and Matt took her hand. Carefully he began to unwrap the bandage until finally he revealed the still inflamed flesh across her palm and around the thumb. His heart lurched, thinking of her in pain. "You're healing nicely. Myers did a great job. You were lucky you didn't have any nerve damage. How is the pain?''

She shrugged her shoulders. ''Hurts a little.''

''Did you take your pills?''

''No, I didn't want to take anything. Not with Erin to think about.''

Matt ripped open a package containing a sterile pad, then began to rewrap the wound.

She winced, and he gentled his touch. ''Sorry.''

She brushed another strand of hair from her face. ''That's okay. It was my fault for dropping the stupid pitcher in the first place.''

''Accidents happen.''

Tara was having trouble breathing from more than the pain in her hand. Why couldn't he just hurry up and finish? With him this near she couldn't stop thinking about last night. How close he'd gotten. She wouldn't let that happen again. Finally the bandage was taped securely and he released her.

Matt seemed to notice her anxiousness. ''That will be less bulky,'' he said. ''But keep your hand in the sling.''

Tara tucked it away. ''For how long?''

''When is your appointment with Dr. Myers?''

''The end of the week.''

''Then keep using the sling until then.''

Great, four more days of being helpless, she thought as she watched Matt close his bag. Then he pointed to the small address book on the table.

''Juanita said you got a package today. Is this from your neighbor?''

''Yes. I was just going through it, hoping to find any names that were familiar to me.''

"May I?" With her nod, he reached for the small leather book. "Did you recognize anyone?"

"One name, Cathy Pennington. She could be Cathy Guthrie. There's a San Diego address and phone number. But all the other names are from Los Angeles." She shook her head. "I don't know any of the other people."

"May I show this to Jim Sloan?"

"Of course." Tara walked to the bed and got the large envelope from Mrs. Lynch. She pulled out a velvet jewelry box that read The Jewel Box across the front. She returned to the table. "Here's the case you wanted. Bri told me Matt had sent her this after she returned to L.A. The last time she heard from him."

He took it from her, and his eyes narrowed as he opened it. Inside was an emerald ring circled in small diamonds. The stone wasn't large, but the setting was beautiful. "I'd say one thing, our thief has great taste." He looked at the box. "I remember this shop. It was on a MasterCard bill I got. I'll have to look it up, but I believe the jewelry store is located downtown."

"So you think he could be from the Santa Cruz area?"

Matt sighed. "Who knows? I've gotten bills from up and down California. Hotels, jewelry stores and restaurants. I guess he was using the card as much as possible until I canceled it."

"Oh, God. What if he's out there seducing other women?"

"Let's hope not. I don't think I can handle any more." He looked at her and stopped. "Sorry, Tara.

What your sister went through was ten times worse than anything this imposter could do to me.''

''My only concern is Erin.''

''It's always the children we can't protect.'' He had a faraway look, as if he were thinking about something totally different. ''So we need to stop him. I'll call Jim and see if he can follow up on these leads. Can I borrow the ring?''

She shrugged. ''Of course. It's yours to keep, since you paid for it.''

''Actually I did pay for the ring, because it came out of a debt account. But it needs to go to Detective Warren as evidence in the crime. Then I think it should go to Erin. A gift from her mother.''

How thoughtful and generous he was, Tara thought. ''Thank you.''

''You're welcome.'' He turned to leave, then stopped at the door. ''We'll talk more at dinner. Six o'clock. You're in for a treat, Juanita is cooking pot roast. Afterward, I'll take you for a walk on the beach, guaranteed to help you sleep.''

Her head was spinning. ''But…Erin.''

''Bring her along. You can strap her into that carrier thing you were wearing that first day in the office. The food and fresh air will do you both some good.''

The silence stretched between them. Then he spoke. ''Look, Tara. There's one other thing I need to talk about with you. Last night.''

She swallowed. ''Last night?''

''I nearly kissed you.'' He ran a hand through his hair, his coffee-colored eyes searching hers. ''I was out of line. But I don't want you worrying about me taking advantage of you.''

So he was regretting it, Tara thought as she nodded. "That's all right. There was no harm done."

"Still, if you're involved with someone back home…"

It would make the situation simpler if she lied. Instead, she said, "No. I'm not involved with anyone."

He looked unconvinced. "That's hard to believe."

"I've been…too busy with college to think about a relationship."

Tara felt the heat spread over her as Matt's gaze assessed her. She found she couldn't move, couldn't breathe.

"The men in Phoenix must be blind."

Heat rushed to her face. "Why don't we just forget about it?"

Matt nodded. "Forgotten."

"I mean the last thing we should do is get…distracted." Why was she rambling? "We don't need any added complications."

He nodded again. "No, we don't." He stared at her for a long moment, his eyes dark and searching.

"Well, dinner will be at six. You and Erin can come to the house any time you're ready."

"Six will be fine." She needed him to leave. "See you then."

Matt stood for a moment wondering what had just happened. He found he wanted to kiss her more now than he had last night. Damn. He grabbed his doctor's bag, headed out the door. Followed the brick path back to the house and entered the kitchen. Juanita was checking the roast in the oven.

"Tara will be here for dinner," Matt announced.

There was a big grin on the housekeeper's face.

"I heard." She pointed to the baby monitor on the table.

Matt bit back a groan, knowing it would be useless to deny anything. "Just don't say anything," he warned.

She shook her head. "Not a word. Just that it's wonderful."

"Nothing happened."

"Almost kissing Tara isn't nothing."

"That's just it, I didn't kiss her. And I'm not going to."

The look in Juanita's eyes spoke volumes. And nothing Matt said was going to change that. His denials were meaningless. He *did* want to kiss Tara.

After dinner, they left the house for their walk. Juanita volunteered to watch Erin. Tara followed Matt along the path, then down the dozen wooden steps to the sandy beach. She stopped to gaze at the sun as it settled over the water. It was magnificent to watch the fiery orange ball illuminate the water, making it look like a sheet of glass. The wind whipped up and blew open the sweatshirt jacket Matt had given her. She tugged on the lapels, held them together and inhaled a combination of the sea air and Matt's scent.

"Are you warm enough?" Matt asked as he came up beside her.

"Yes, this feels wonderful."

He smiled. "I thought you'd prefer the heat since you're from Phoenix."

"Sometimes you can't choose where you live." She looked at the surf.

"You could always move. I did. My family is from the Midwest. The minute I came out here, I knew I couldn't live anywhere else.'' His eyes brightened, showing golden flecks. "Now that you're a teacher, you could find a job anywhere.''

"I've always lived in Phoenix.'' But was that reason enough not to spread her wings? she wondered.

His dark gaze held her captive, making it impossible to keep her thoughts focused. But she had to think clearly. A man like Matt Landers could hurt her. He wasn't her type. He was a heart surgeon in a fancy hospital. "Besides, in Phoenix I have friends…close friends.''

He cocked an eyebrow. "But no close men friends?''

Tara shook her head. She could count on her fingers the dates she'd had in the past few years. "I told you earlier that there wasn't anyone in my life. It's not exactly easy for a single mother to meet an acceptable man, who wants to be an instant father.''

"Guess not,'' Matt said. His blond hair blew in the wind. He seemed to be at home near the sea. "Come on, I promised you a walk. Take off your shoes.''

She toed off her tennis shoes, and he did the same. He grabbed her good hand, leading her to the wet sand where they strolled along the surf.

The next ten minutes were spent in a comfortable silence. Matt liked that about Tara. She didn't need to always be talking. And he needed quiet. This was how he cleared his head of the pressures of his job. He liked holding her hand, the warmth of her slender fingers intertwined with his. It made him think of other things. He quickly cut off the direction of his thoughts and asked, "Is this the first time you've been to the beach?''

"The very first.''

"Well, then, you should at least be christened."
Careful of her sling, he swept her into his arms and
carried her into the water.

She gasped and insisted he put her down. He only
smiled, then continued to walk through the waves.
She grabbed him around his neck and held on. He
could feel the silkiness of her hair against his neck
and the curve of her soft body against his. Whoa.
Bad idea. Finally he set her on her feet in the water.

"Oh, it's freezing." Tara danced in the foamy
surf, then turned to shore. When she stumbled, Matt
hurried to her rescue. He lifted her before she got
too wet. But he paid the price as her body meshed
with his. Desire raced through him.

Tara froze, and so did he. He wanted nothing more
than to lean down and take her mouth, but he knew
he wouldn't stop there. He caught the intense look
in her large eyes. He slowly eased her away from his
heated body.

"Tara, I'm…" He wanted to ask her so many
questions, but he had no right. They had only been
thrown together because of circumstances. The best
thing to do was put a stop to the temptation.

Regaining his common sense, he released her. "I
think it's time we went in."

With her nod, he led her to the stairs. Silently they
retrieved their shoes then started up the steps. Matt
knew that spending so much time together could only
lead to where they didn't need to go.

He turned and watched the slim woman climb, her
gaze leveled on his. *No, don't think about how she
felt in your arms, or how the rich green of her eyes
makes you forget everything.*

"Your name came up at the hospital today," he

said as he turned toward the surf, letting the sea spray cool him off.

"By who?" Tara asked as she stopped to brush the wet sand from her feet.

"Charlene mentioned how much she'd like to have you work at the center."

"How can I with my hand...and Erin."

"She's willing to take you, wound and all. Charlene is even willing to work around your schedule, and Erin can go with you. She was impressed with your ideas, especially for the field trips."

Tara was speechless. She didn't know what to say. The money would come in handy. The money it was costing her to stay here was putting a big dent in her budget.

"Surely she knows I'll only be around for a few weeks," Tara said.

"I told her you needed to be back in Phoenix by mid-August."

"I wasn't planning on staying that long." It would be dangerous for her to get too involved.

He looked around before settling his gaze on her. "I guess that all depends on how quickly we find the thief. Jim has the names in the address book." He shrugged. "And I have no problem with you and Erin staying in the cottage as long as you want. Why not spend some of the summer at the beach instead of in the Phoenix heat? Unless you have other plans."

Tara had decided she would stay until her stitches were removed and not much past that. But with a job...that could change things. "My only plans were to come to Santa Cruz."

When they arrived at the cottage, Juanita greeted them. "I've put Erin down for the night, and she's already sound asleep.'' The older woman left with a smile.

Matt stood on the porch. ''Well, I'll say good-night, too. I have to be at the hospital early.''

''Thank you for the walk,'' Tara said, grateful he didn't want to come inside.

He hesitated. ''Should I tell Charlene you're interested in the job?''

''Let me think about it.'' Working at the hospital would definitely mean seeing more of Matt. And she found she liked that idea too much.

''Sounds good. Good night,'' he called over his shoulder.

Tara watched as he walked to the house and disappeared inside. She couldn't take her eyes off his imposing figure, those broad shoulders, as he disappeared into the house. She closed the door and sagged against it with a long, tired sigh. This was bad. She was developing a crush on Matt Landers. With every passing day, she was becoming more and more confused by this man. And the last thing she needed was to allow herself to get caught up by his kindness. His bedroom eyes. The tenderness of his touch. She closed her eyes and thought of the way he'd held her on the beach....

No! She pushed away from the door. Men like Matt Landers didn't fall for schoolteachers from Phoenix. No, she wasn't the daydreamer Bri had been. She couldn't let herself be fooled, let her emotions keep her from thinking clearly—from protecting Erin's future.

But Dr. Landers made it damn hard to stay cool.

## Chapter Seven

The next afternoon, there was more bad news. Matt sat in his office, on the phone with Jim Sloan.

"I'm sorry, Matt. So far most of the phone numbers in the address book have been dead ends. Some have been disconnected, others changed with no new numbers."

"Well, keep trying," Matt insisted. There had to be a clue in there somewhere.

"We're still checking out the hotel in Acapulco. So far we've discovered there was a Dr. Matthew Landers registered there the last week in March and the first week in April. I'm going to fly down and check with some of the employees to see if I can get a description of the man."

Matt let out a long breath, remembering the call he'd gotten from a bank that morning about a car he'd supposedly leased and was delinquent on the payments. Matt spent thirty minutes explaining the situation to the car dealer. Then he referred the man to the fraud division at the police department. This whole experience had been nothing short of humiliating. He gripped the telephone receiver more tightly. "In the meantime he's still out there, using my name, destroying my credit rating and reputation."

"Yeah, this guy has been an expert at covering his tracks," Jim said. "But he's going to slip up sooner or later, and we'll nail him."

"Let's just hope it's not later," Matt mumbled, wondering if there would be anything left to take from him by then.

"I do have some good news," Jim said. "I've checked out your Ms. Tara McNeal. Everything she told us was true. She is from Phoenix and attended Arizona State University in Mesa. She graduated with a degree in elementary education and did her student teaching last fall at Price Elementary, then was asked to stay on as a kindergarten teacher. During most of her time in college she worked for a small family-owned restaurant called Hometown Grill."

Matt had known all along that Tara was telling him the truth, but he'd had no choice but to check her out. With this crook on the loose, he wasn't able to trust anyone. He hated it, but being cautious was his way of life these days.

"Now, her younger sister was a different story," Sloan went on. "Briana McNeal was a little more adventurous. She liked a faster-paced life. She had several jobs in L.A., mostly as a cocktail waitress. She worked some of the exclusive clubs in the area, the Gentleman's Club, Studio Hollywood and the

Jazzy Club. So she made pretty good money as a hostess." There was a pause. "Of course, if she was into anything else, she could have made even more money...a lot more."

"I don't think I need to hear anything else. Just put together the file. I can look it over later." Matt hated the feeling that he was gathering information that would hurt Tara and Erin.

"Okay, I'll drop the file off at your office before I catch my plane. I'll call you when I get back."

"Thanks, Jim. I'm going to check out the jewelry store in Monterey. Maybe they'll have something for me."

Matt hung up the phone, knowing all he could do was sit and wait. Wait, while Tara and Erin were living only about a hundred feet from his door. Wait, while every day, he was getting more and more attached to the two of them. He hated knowing he could never be the man they needed him to be. Tara wanted the thing he could never give her—a family.

He stood, went to the window behind his desk and looked at the rolling surf.

Dammit, it wasn't fair that his life had been turned upside down. It wasn't fair that he was being tempted with a beautiful woman and a child he could never claim. He rubbed his forehead. What had he done to deserve this?

The intercom sounded, and Judy informed him he had a patient in exam room one. Matt thanked her and took off down the hall. At the door, he smiled as he checked the name on the chart, then walked inside.

Eight-year-old Danny Malone sat on the exam table. The dark-haired boy had a smile that lit up his large brown eyes, and there was a healthy glow to his olive skin. Only his full, rounded face, the evidence of the antirejection medication he took, and a faint scar down the center of his chest gave evidence he'd had a heart transplant six years ago.

"Hey, kiddo." They exchanged a high five.

"Hi, Dr. Matt."

Matt glanced at the boy's father. "Hi, Nick." Then he looked at Danny. "Couldn't ditch the old man, huh?"

Danny laughed. "No, he brought me from baseball practice."

"How is it going?"

The boy puffed out his chest. "I'm playing first base. Dad's been practicing with me."

Nick smiled. "What can I say, my son's a natural. And he's been working hard." A worried look appeared on Nick's face. He approached the exam table. "I thought we should make sure Danny's not overdoing it. He seemed to get awfully winded this morning."

"Dad, we were running laps. All the guys were breathing hard."

Matt knew that Nick had come a long way in letting his son be a normal kid. He slipped his stethoscope in his ears as he winked at Danny. That was the signal Matt and Danny had worked out long ago when Nick dragged his son into the office every time his child sneezed. A few years ago, Matt had explained to Danny that his father worried so much because he cared about him. As it turned out, it had been Cari who convinced Nick to allow his eldest son to be normal. Or as close to normal as any kid with a heart transplant could hope to be.

Matt listened to Danny's chest. His heartbeat was strong. It was another of those miracles that, as a doctor, Matt never took for granted, the health of his young patients. "Yeah, it's beating, all right," he said aloud.

Danny giggled.

"Here, you listen." He let the boy listen for himself.

"Yep, Dad, it's beating. See, I'm okay. Now, can we go home?"

Nick's expression wasn't as cheerful as his son's. Matt could see he had concerns. "Danny, why don't you put your shirt on and go help Judy with her computer? I'm sure she has a bunch of questions for you."

Danny jumped down from the table. "Okay, but Dad, listen to Dr. Matt. He won't let anything bad happen to me." Surprising Matt, Danny hugged him, then ran out the door.

Matt folded his arms. "You've got a pretty wise kid there."

"I know, but I can't help it that I worry," Nick began. "Now that he's older, all he thinks about is sports. Don't you remember how rough it is out there?"

"I wasn't much of an athlete in school, but a little baseball has been good for him. And Danny wants to play. He wants to be one of the guys." Matt looked at Danny's file and scanned his last set of tests. "There's nothing here that indicates any problem." He looked at his friend. "So don't create any, Nick."

Nick moved around the small room like a caged animal. "This is so hard. Every time I look at that boy, I realize what a miracle he is. It's just…I don't want anything to happen to him.''

Suddenly the image of Erin came into Matt's mind. A strange protective urge clutched his heart. He pushed it away and directed his comments to his friend. ''I know, Nick. Danny's special to me, too. But life has no guarantees, so let the kid be a kid.''

Nick drew a long breath and released it. ''Easier said than done.''

Matt slapped him on the back. ''I don't think it's ever easy. But I'm here if you need reassurance.''

''Thanks.'' Nick sighed. ''How about you? How are you and your houseguests getting along?''

Matt wondered if Nick was playing matchmaker or just making idle conversation. ''Fine. I hardly ever see them.'' Which was only a half truth.

Nick gave him a doubtful look. ''So how long will she be staying?''

''As long as it takes,'' he said, but that didn't seem to convince his friend. ''Look, Nick. I'm the one who needs Tara to stay here. I'm desperate to straighten out my life.''

Nick nodded slowly. ''This is all so strange. It's as if someone is purposely trying to wreck your life. Have you made any enemies lately?''

Matt leaned against the table. ''I've been racking my brain, but I can't come up with anything in particular. As a doctor, I'm vulnerable, and I hate to think someone out there thinks I was purposely negligent. If so, I want a chance to defend myself.''

Nick studied him for a minute. ''So you think that Tara McNeal isn't involved in any of this?''

Matt shook his head. ''I think Briana, Tara and little Erin were just pawns in this mess.''

There was a knock on the door, and Cari Malone poked her head inside. "Is this conversation for men only?"

Nick lit up as he drew his wife inside and into his arms. "No, it's just Matt's usual lecture on being overprotective."

She looked at her husband, her expression pure love. "Well, if you're going to have a fault, that's one I can live with." She stood on her toes and kissed him tenderly.

Matt cleared his throat loudly. "You two should get a room."

Nick broke off the kiss and grinned. "You should try it. The right woman would do wonders for your attitude."

"There's nothing wrong with my attitude," Matt said as his gaze went to the doorway and found Tara.

Matt felt his whole body go on alert for the pretty redhead. She wore a long skirt with a white T-shirt and a wine-colored vest. Her hair curled around her face, and her ears were adorned with hoop earrings. She looked fresh…and sexy.

He stood up straighter. "Tara."

She smiled shyly. "Cari gave me a lift to the hospital. It's okay, isn't it? I came in to talk with Charlene."

"Sure." He felt the heat rush to his face seeing Nick's knowing grin.

Then his friend tugged on his wife's hand and they headed for the door. "Guess it's time to take our kid and leave," Nick said. Cari stopped her husband's departure to ask, "Matt, can you take Tara home?"

"Sure, no problem," he said. "If she doesn't mind hanging around for about an hour."

"I don't mind, but I want to call Juanita."

"Use the phone in my office," Matt suggested.

Tara started down the hall. Cari stopped her. "Why don't you guys come over this weekend and we'll have a barbecue? Matt, you haven't seen Matthew in a while. Don't answer now. Think about it." She tugged on her husband's hand, and they were gone.

Matt spent a quiet moment wondering if the invitation was making Tara uncomfortable. "You mustn't feel obligated to go. Cari likes you—"

"And I like her," Tara said. "I was introduced to Danny in the waiting room, and I'm anxious to meet Krissy and Matthew. I hear your namesake is quite a handful."

Matt was surprised. "He's pure boy," he said proudly. "A handsome devil, too."

Tara laughed, and Matt felt a tightening in his gut. What this woman did to him should be illegal. He needed to get out of the small confines of the exam room before he did something foolish.

"Do you have to go up and see Charlene?"

Tara shook her head and smiled shyly. "No, I've already been to the center. As of thirty minutes ago, I'm an employee of Riverhaven."

Tara's first day working at the day-care center had been a long and exhausting one. For both her and Erin.

Too bad all the physical activity hadn't been enough to put Tara to sleep, as it had Erin. Tara raised her head off the pillow and looked at the clock. It was after one o'clock. She groaned, closed her eyes and listened to the wind whistling past the cottage windows. It was stronger tonight than it had been before. Maybe that was what was making her nervous.

She'd hated wind ever since she'd gotten caught outside in a bad storm on her way home from school. She took cover in a garage that had been left open. She recalled getting soaked, but it had been the fierce wind that threatened to blow her away that had terrified her.

Once again the wind whipped around the porch and battered the windows. Snuggling under the blankets, Tara listened to the creaking of the cottage and wondered if the structure could stand the force. A patter of heavy rain struck the roof and windows. All at once the rain began to come down in hard, heavy sheets.

Tara knew she wouldn't sleep. She got up, put on her robe and went to check on Erin. The baby was still sleeping, so Tara checked all the windows, then turned on the light over the stove. She began filling the tea pot, then noticed something dripping from overhead. She looked up to see water coming in from the roof. Great—a leak! When she went to get a pan there was another strong gust of wind and a cracking sound, then a loud crash nearby.

Tara screamed and ran to the crib. She grabbed Erin. A tree branch had broken through the window, and shattered glass lay across the double bed where she'd been sleeping moments ago. The baby began to cry as the light flickered and went out. *Don't panic,* Tara told herself. She fumbled for the blanket on the back of the sofa, draped the baby protectively and started for the door.

Matt burst in. "Tara! Tara, where are you?"

"Oh, Matt," she cried and hurried to the shadowed figure in the doorway. She sought safety in his arms. "A tree came through the window," she wailed.

"Let's get you and Erin into the house." He took the baby and tried to soothe her cries. "It's okay, sweetie. I got you."

He draped the blanket tightly around the baby and opened the door. The wind hit them full force. "Come on," he called over his shoulder, then took Tara's hand. Fighting the wind, they started for the house, hurrying across the nearly flooded backyard as heavy rain pounded down around them. Finally they got inside the house.

Matt continued to soothe Erin. "Shh, princess. You're safe now. I'm here to take care of you."

Within seconds the baby quieted. Matt looked at Tara. "Are you all right?"

She was still shaking from the incident. "Just scared. The wind was so strong and then the crash..." Her words drifted off when she realized Matt was half naked. His glorious chest was bare, and he wore only a pair of jeans. "I thought the whole roof was going—"

"It's all right, it's over. Come on. We'll get you both dry."

Juanita rushed into the room carrying towels, speaking Spanish. "Is everyone okay?"

"Yeah, but no thanks to the big tree that decided to make an entrance into the cottage," Matt said, wiping his face on the towel."

"Want me to take the baby?" Juanita offered.

"No need," he said. "Tara, you go with Juanita and get dried off. I can take care of Erin."

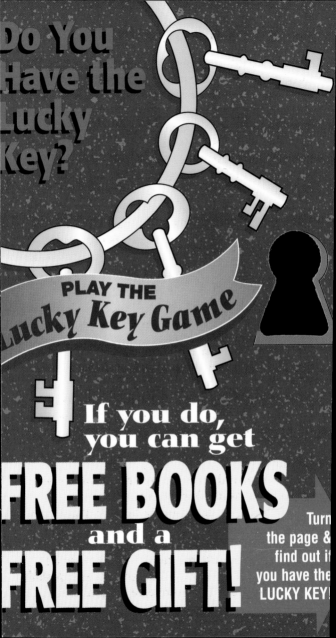

# PLAY THE
## Lucky Key Game
### and get

## HOW TO PLAY:

1. With a coin, carefully scratch off gold area at the right. Then check the claim chart to see what we have for you — **2 FREE BOOKS** and a **FREE GIFT** — **ALL YOURS FREE!**

2. Send back the card and you'll receive two brand-new Silhouette Special Edition® novels. These books have a cover price of $4.50 each in the U.S. and $5.25 each in Canada, but they are yours to keep absolutely free.

3. There's no catch. You're under no obligation to buy anything. We charge nothing —ZERO — for your first shipment. And you don't have to make any minimum number of purchases — not even one!

4. The fact is, thousands of readers enjoy receiving books by mail from the Silhouette Reader Service™. They enjoy the convenience of home delivery...they like getting the best new novels at discount prices, BEFORE they're available in stores...and they love their *Heart to Heart* subscriber newsletter featuring author news, horoscopes, recipes, book reviews and much more!

5. We hope that after receiving your free books you'll want to remain a subscriber. But the choice is yours — to continue or cancel, any time at all! So why not take us up on our invitation, with no risk of any kind. You'll be glad you did!

# YOURS FREE!
## A SURPRISE MYSTERY GIFT

We can't tell you what it is...but we're sure you'll like it! A
## FREE GIFT–
just for playing the LUCKY KEY game!

# FREE GIFTS!

## NO COST! NO OBLIGATION TO BUY!
## NO PURCHASE NECESSARY!

## PLAY THE
# Lucky Key Game

Scratch gold area with a coin.
Then check below to see the gifts you get!

335 SDL C4FL
235 SDL C4FG

## YES! I have scratched off the gold area. Please send me the 2 Free books and gift for which I qualify. I understand I am under no obligation to purchase any books, as explained on the back and on the opposite page.

NAME                                          (PLEASE PRINT CLEARLY)

ADDRESS

APT.#                              CITY

STATE/PROV.                                   ZIP/POSTAL CODE

2 free books plus a mystery gift          1 free book

2 free books          Try Again!

(S-SE-0S-07/00)

# The Silhouette Reader Service™ — Here's how it works:

Accepting your 2 free books and gift places you under no obligation to buy anything. You may keep the books and gift an return the shipping statement marked "cancel." If you do not cancel, about a month later we'll send you 6 additional nove and bill you just $3.80 each in the U.S., or $4.21 each in Canada, plus 25¢ delivery per book and applicable taxes if any.*
That's the complete price and — compared to cover prices of $4.50 each in the U.S. and $5.25 each in Canada — it's qui
a bargain! You may cancel at any time, but if you choose to continue, every month we'll send you 6 more books, which y
may either purchase at the discount price or return to us and cancel your subscription.

*Terms and prices subject to change without notice. Sales tax applicable in N.Y. Canadian residents will be charged
applicable provincial taxes and GST.

"I'll make up the bed in the guest room," the housekeeper said as she headed down the hall.

"You don't have to," Tara insisted, unable to control her shivering. "We can just stay on the sofa till morning."

Matt cuddled the baby against his bare chest. "You might as well sleep in a bed. It looks like you'll be staying for awhile."

"Why?"

"Because you can't live in a place that's missing windows and maybe part of a roof."

"But…but surely they can patch it up tomorrow."

Matt took his eyes off the baby long enough to glance outside. "This is a freak storm, Tara. Rare for June. It will be difficult to get someone to come out after a heavy rain. It might be a week before they can do the repairs. I hope none of your things were damaged."

"Just the bed. Glass broke all over it."

He studied her for a long time, his dark eyes intent on her face. "But you and Erin didn't get hurt. Nothing else matters."

Tara tried to control her trembling, thinking about what had nearly happened. "Then we should go to a motel."

"Not tonight," he said. "The road to the highway is probably already covered in an inch of mud. Now stop arguing. You're freezing."

Tara's heart raced even faster, knowing Matt would be so close. No, she couldn't stay here.

"I know you're shaken up from the storm, but after a night's sleep, you'll feel better," he said.

"I don't want to put you out."

He smiled at her. "Why? We have Juanita as a chaperone."

Tara felt her face flush, embarrassed that he didn't seem the least bit bothered that she would be staying at his house. "I'm not worried," she denied.

"Good. Now, come on. You need to get out of those wet clothes. Then I'll change the bandage on your hand." Carrying Erin, Matt started down the hall.

Tara looked at her soaked cotton robe and night-shirt. They definitely didn't leave much to the imagination. She quickly folded her arms across her chest and followed him.

Matt turned into a large room with the sky-blue walls where Juanita kept a crib for Erin. A soft light was on next to the double bed. The housekeeper was busy smoothing out the fresh sheets.

"You don't have to do that, Juanita." Tara came to her side. "I can make the bed."

"Change those clothes, or you'll be sick."

"I can't. Everything is in the cottage."

Juanita shook her head. "It's no wonder, having to run out into the stormy night. You were lucky you weren't hurt." The woman blessed herself. "I'll find you something." The housekeeper was gone and back again in seconds carrying a pair of men's burgundy pajamas. "One of Dr. Matt's many Christmas gifts."

"These are new," Tara said.

Matt exchanged a smile with Juanita. "And they'll stay new because I don't wear pajamas."

Tara blushed, trying not to picture what Matt wore or didn't wear to bed.

The housekeeper went to her boss and took Erin

from him. "You might consider sleeping in something now that you have female guests in the house." She carried the baby to the portable crib. Erin gave a soft whine as Juanita changed her diaper.

Matt watched the housekeeper tend to the baby, knowing close quarters with Tara wasn't a good idea.

"Such a sweetheart. She's already settling in for the night," Juanita said. "But I'll get her a bottle just in case." She hurried from the room.

"Change into those dry clothes," Matt said to Tara. When she hesitated, he said, "I'll watch the baby."

Clutching the pajamas, Tara made her way into the connecting bathroom. With the click of the door, Matt walked to the crib. Great. Now they were closer than ever—closer than it was safe for them to be. He glanced at the little girl looking at him with big, trusting eyes. She gave a weak cry, and he smiled. "I don't blame you for being upset. It's been a crazy night. And it's going to get crazier before long." How was he supposed to sleep with Tara McNeal down the hall?

"But you, my little cutie, I wouldn't mind if you stayed a while." Erin reached out and took hold of his finger. "Just be careful with my heart when you have to leave me." And from experience, Matt knew they would leave. A rush of loneliness overcame him, and he stroked little Erin's cheek. For the first time in a long time, he allowed himself to wish things could be different.

The bathroom door opened and Tara walked in. He swallowed hard. She was tall, but with her delicate frame she couldn't quite take up the slack in the extra tall pajamas. She looked innocent yet sexy.

Damn, he was in trouble.

They both stood there until Tara spoke. "I really appreciate you letting us invade your house. I promise not to cause too much inconvenience."

"I want you and Erin to make yourselves at home for as long as you need to stay. You know I'm gone for long periods at a time, anyway. You'll be good company for Juanita."

"Thank you."

"You're welcome," he whispered. "Sit down on the bed." When she looked startled, he bit back a grin. "I'm only going to change your bandage."

He went into the bedroom and came out with some sterile pads and tape. His attention on his task, he swiftly removed the wet bandage and examined her stitches. All these agonizing minutes, he was trying not to think about how close she was and about the softness of her skin. Her intoxicating scent drifted around his head, teasing him, causing sensual thoughts about one attractive redhead.

Then he made his biggest mistake. He raised his gaze to hers and suddenly became mesmerized by her incredible emerald eyes. He couldn't break the hold, nor did he want to. Knowing she was going to be sleeping in his pajamas nearly drove him crazy, all that silky material against her bare skin.

Ah, hell. Here he was in the same room with a baby and all he could think about was what it would be like to take Tara into his bed and to make slow, easy love to her all night long.

He bit back a groan as he watched the pulse pounding in her neck. She was feeling it, too.

Juanita burst into the room carrying a bottle. She smiled. "Well, I see everyone's ready for bed."

* * *

It was an endless night. The rain continued to pound for the next hour. As Erin slept peacefully, Tara tossed and turned, unable to get Matt out of her head. The way he looked at her, the way he touched her. Staying here, at the house, was going to be trouble.

She climbed out of bed and walked to the kitchen. She found a glass and got some ice and poured water over it, then went into the living room and watched the rain.

"It's been awhile since we've had a storm like this."

Tara gasped as she swung around to find Matt. "Oh, I didn't know you were awake."

He crossed the room. He was wearing a robe over a pair of sweatpants, but even in the dimly lit room she could see his chest was bare.

"I didn't mean to startle you." He studied her. "Can't you sleep?"

She shook her head. "Having a tree crash through my window has a tendency to make me a little restless. But please don't feel you have to stay up for me." In fact, she'd rather have him far away.

"I can't sleep, either. I guess it's all the excitement." He stepped closer. "I was on my way out to the cottage to bring you both to the house when I heard the crash. I saw the tree fall. God, I was so afraid something happened...." His gaze met hers. He reached out and touched her cheek.

Tara couldn't help herself. She leaned into his palm. "I was so scared, too," she whispered. "Thank you for coming to our rescue."

Matt told himself the smart thing to do was to turn

around and head back to bed. Alone. To stay away from this woman. Instead, he bent his head toward hers. He ached to know what it was like to hold her in his arms, to taste her. One touch of her lips, and he knew the answer. First came the rush of sensation. Even though the kiss was slow and tentative there was a definite fire ignited between them.

She tasted of mint and a sweetness he couldn't describe. He only knew he wanted more. He had to have more. His hands cupped her face, and he teased her lips with his tongue. When she moaned, he pushed inside. Their passion soared as he plunged deeper, wanting—needing to taste all of her. He drew her against him and heard her soft, whimpering sound.

Her hand went to his chest. He shuddered, relishing her warmth against his skin. At first he thought she was going to push him away, then to his relief, she traced her fingers along his sensitive flesh, sending slivers of heat through him, making him rock hard. When she wrapped her arm around his neck and pressed her body into his, he nearly went crazy. His fingers dug into her hair, holding her captive as his tongue delved deep, relaying his need. His hands skimmed down her silken-covered back, learning her curves, aching to be inside her.

He raised his head and drew a needed breath. The light in the hall illuminated the questioning look in her eyes.

"Oh, Tara." It was all he could say. Unable to stop himself, he began teasing her lips with nibbling kisses, then took her mouth again.

This time Tara became aggressive as her tongue danced with his, driving him crazy with a need he hadn't satisfied in so long. He came alive, wanting the pleasure she was offering. When his hand slipped under the pajama top and found the bare skin at her waist, she whispered his name.

Slowly the kiss ended as he gripped her shoulders. ''Tara,'' he said, his voice fading away. But through the haze of desire he knew this had to stop. Any further and they'd both regret it. ''We have to stop.''

Tara started to speak, but Matt silenced her with his finger against that sweet mouth of hers. He didn't want any words to spoil what they had shared. Then he forced himself to turn and walk away, knowing there was no way he'd be able to sleep.

But for one night, he would allow himself to dream about the beautiful woman he'd held in his arms. For one night he would dream of what he knew he could never have.

Matt was gone the next morning when Tara got up at seven. Grateful but a little disappointed, she went to the cottage and surveyed the damage. Across her bed was a large tree branch, and scattered glass was everywhere. Tara shivered, thinking about what could have happened if she had been sleeping. She glanced at the baby bed. It had avoided any damage. Tara had an overwhelming urge to cry, which was unlike her. She was a survivor. She'd always been able to handle anything thrown her way. But now she had to think about Erin and what was best for the child.

She went to the kitchenette and sank down in the chair at the table and buried her face in her hands. The tears came fast and free. Tara hadn't allowed herself to cry when Bri died—she had too many other things to think about— She had Erin to care for and ever since, she'd been too busy to let herself grieve. Now tears flooded her eyes and sobs racked her tired body.

For the first time since Erin's birth, Tara was letting her fears surface. What was she to do? Where was she to go? Stay here and find Erin's father? Her thoughts turned to Matt and the kisses they'd shared in the middle of the night. She groaned, remembering how she practically threw herself at the man.

No, she couldn't let herself fall for him. He didn't want to be saddled with her or the baby. He needed her for now, to find the man who'd disrupted his world. Then she would be shipped back to Phoenix...and without a man in her life. Again.

"So keep your head, girl. Don't let a good-looking doctor persuade you otherwise," she said. "Stay at the house, help Matt find this man, then go home."

Wiping her tears, she stood with new determination and began gathering her clothes. The cottage door opened, and she swung around to find Matt.

Matt had no idea what brought him to the cottage. He had patients to see, but he knew he couldn't go on without talking with Tara.

"I called a contractor this morning. He'll be out tomorrow afternoon to start the work. It shouldn't take more than a few days. Then you can have your privacy back."

She didn't look him in the eye. "I guess we'll be hanging around for a while. Unless you...changed your mind about wanting us to stay. We can go to a motel."

He walked to her. "Yes, I want you to stay here. This house is big enough to keep out of everyone's way. Besides, you can't handle Erin by yourself. So looks like we need each other.''

"I just wish I could be more help to you.''

"You're doing a lot. Jim's still going through the names in the address book. And you need closure so you and Erin can move on.''

Tara nodded. She knew Matt was right. She had to put Briana to rest and make a life for her new daughter. And that could only happen if the man who fathered Erin was found.

"Besides, Erin loves being here,'' he said. "She's crazy about Juanita. And Juanita…well, I think you know how she feels.''

They were all getting attached. But sooner or later, she had to return to Phoenix. "I do have my job at the hospital, and I'd hate to run out on Charlene.'' And she could use the extra money for paying her bills.

"Then why not stay and work at the day-care? If we're lucky, we could find this guy, then you can tell him that he has a daughter. Isn't that what Briana wanted?''

"Yes, but I don't think my sister expected her baby's father to be a thief.''

From experience Matt knew you don't always get what you want. "Bri had to know that *her* Matt Landers wasn't the nicest guy. After all, he ran out on her. But believe me, children will want to know where and who they came from. It may not seem important now, but in a few years it will, when Erin starts asking about her father.'' Matt's heart tightened. "Trust me, Tara, I know this.

"I was adopted by wonderful people, but ever since I was old enough to ask questions, I wanted to know more about my biological parents. And my adoptive parents didn't have the answers. Don't do that to Erin.''

Her gaze met his, her eyes brimming with compassion.

''But I'm staying in your house,'' she began. ''What about what happened last night?''

Matt drew a long breath. ''If you're talking about the kiss, I know I was way out of line. I believe the storm had something to do with it. You were vulnerable, and I took advantage. I'm sorry, Tara. It won't happen again.''

She stood silent for a long time, then nodded.

His pager went off, and he glanced at the number. ''It's Jim Sloan.'' He went to the phone and dialed. After a short conversation he returned to her.

''Jim said he found an old neighbor of Bri's in Los Angeles. Supposedly, they were friends. A Lori Green. She and Bri used to work together. She won't talk with Jim, but she said she'd talk with Bri's sister.''

Matt could see that Tara was intrigued, then she looked at her injured hand.

''Your stitches come out on Friday. You still have to be careful, but I think by then you'll be able to use your hand. Will you fly down with me?''

''What about Erin and my work?''

''If Juanita can watch her, are you willing to go this weekend?''

Tara wasn't making any snap decisions. He found he liked that. She had common sense. He'd thought he did, too, but after last night, he wasn't so sure. This woman had him completely off center.

''Okay, I'll go.''

"Great. I'll make reservations for Saturday morning. We can be back that evening." His excitement began to build. "This could be the break we need."

This trip could also be a huge mistake…unless he found a way to keep things strictly business. Looking at Tara, he suddenly realized that keeping his desire under control could prove even more difficult than tracking a clever thief.

## Chapter Eight

The plane landed at LAX. Within thirty minutes they had a rental car and were headed to Hollywood.

The area wasn't bad, Tara thought, recalling the awful conditions Bri had lived in the last few months of her life. Matt parked the car in front of a four-story apartment building. Jim was waiting for them out front.

"Miss Green is home. I called her about an hour ago and told her you'd be coming today."

Matt helped Tara out of the car. "Let's just hope Tara can get some helpful information."

Jim nodded as they went up the steps. Jim pushed the apartment number and was answered by Lori Green, who gave them access to the building. They rode the elevator to the second floor. A young blond woman wearing faded jeans and a red T-shirt waited for them by her door.

"Ms. Green?" Sloan asked.

She gave both men the once-over and smiled, then turned her attention to the only other woman present.

"So you're Tara."

Tara nodded.

"Bri used to talk about you."

Tara tensed. "You were friends with my sister?"

The blonde pointed to the door across the hall. "She lived over there for nearly a year."

"When did she move out?" Jim asked.

Lori stared at him. "About ten months ago. That was something you could have found out from the landlord, and I'm only taking questions from Tara McNeal." She opened her apartment door. "Would you like to come in?"

"Yes, I would. I'd like to know everything about my sister." Before Tara went inside, she looked at the two men. "Why don't you go downstairs and wait for me?"

Matt took her hands. "Will you be all right?"

She smiled. "I'll be fine."

"Here's a list of questions to ask," Jim Sloan said as he slipped her a small notebook. Then both men walked to the elevator.

Tara entered the comfortable-looking apartment with a spacious living room and an attached kitchenette.

"Can I get you something to drink? Coffee? Soda?"

"If you're having coffee that would be nice."

Lori poured coffee into two mugs then took them to the table and offered Tara a seat.

"I'm sorry that I didn't talk with the PI, but I've had some bad experience with people snooping into other people's business. I don't like being caught in the middle, and Bri was my friend. I'm sorry, I had no idea she was sick.''

''When was the last time you saw her?''

''In September, when she moved.''

''Did you know she went to Mexico?''

The blonde took a sip of coffee, then nodded. ''Yeah, that's all she talked about. She and another friend named Cathy were going to spend ten days down in Acapulco. I really envied her but I couldn't afford to go.''

''Do you know Cathy's last name? Was it Guthrie?''

Lori frowned. ''No, it wasn't Guthrie. Let me think. It was…Pennington. That's it, Pennington. I didn't know her very well. From what I remember Bri and her moved to L.A. together. Later, Cathy married a Marine. I think the reason they went to Mexico was that her husband had shipped out overseas.''

Tara glanced at the notebook and asked another question. ''Did Bri tell you about the man she met in Mexico?''

Lori leaned back in her chair and smiled. ''Are you kidding? That's all I heard about for weeks after she came home. Matt this, Matt that.''

''Matt Landers?''

She snapped her fingers. ''That's it. And he was some kind of doctor. A heart surgeon.''

Tara nodded. ''That's what he told her.'' She felt so bad for her sister. *Why is it so hard to find someone worthy to love?*

''I had a feeling he was too good to be true. I bet

he fed her a bunch of bull. What happened, did he have a wife?''

''No, the man who said he was Dr. Matt Landers really wasn't him.'' Tara didn't want to say too much. ''Did you ever see a picture of this man?''

Lori nodded. ''Bri showed me one. Not bad looking. I'd probably look at him twice.''

Tara hadn't found any pictures at Bri's place. ''Could you describe him?''

''He was tanned, with blond hair and brown eyes.''

Tara swallowed before she asked the one question she couldn't help but ask. ''Did he look anything like that blond man I was just with?''

Lori looked confused for a moment, then finally shook her head. ''No, they're not the same person. The man in the picture was only a few inches taller than Bri, maybe five ten. And his hair was a darker blond. His face was longer. There wasn't a cleft in his chin, either.''

Tara knew in her heart that Matt hadn't been in Mexico with her sister, but she still felt relieved. ''Can you tell me why Bri moved from here?''

''She said she got a job in the valley.'' Lori said. ''But now I think she was going to look for this guy.'' She shook her head. ''What a bastard.''

Tara felt the same way. ''Thank you, Lori. You've been a big help.'' She wrote down Matt's number, and hers in Phoenix. ''If you remember anything else will you call me?''

Lori nodded, then walked Tara to the door. But before Tara could leave, Lori stopped her. ''When Bri and I used to talk, especially late at night, your name came up a lot. I know the two of you had argued over the years, but it's a fact that your sister loved you. Bri just thought she couldn't live up to your expectations.''

Tara blinked back the tears in her eyes. "I just wanted her to have a good life."

"She knew that." Lori was also tearing up. "Bri's lucky you're around to raise her little girl."

Tara was the one who was lucky to have Erin. "Sometimes we're blessed with second chances." She turned and headed for the elevator, trying to keep from running—running away from all the things she couldn't take back, or do over, or make right. She had so many regrets and if onlys. All she could do was follow through with Bri's wish to find Erin's father.

She opened the door to the front stoop and saw Matt. With a choked sob, she ran into his arms. Everything she'd been holding back surfaced, and she began to cry.

Tara burrowed into the security of Matt's strong arms. With his warmth surrounding her like a comforting blanket, for once she felt protected, cherished. She wanted to stay there forever, but knew it was only temporary. That's the way it had always been for her. Everything in her life had been temporary.

She pulled from Matt's embrace and wiped her face with a handkerchief he gave her. "I'm sorry."

"No need to be sorry," he assured her. "This had to be hard on you."

"I didn't think that it would bring back so many memories. Lori told me that Bri used to talk about things…family things. About me."

Tara glanced at Jim, who was eagerly waiting for the details. She handed him the notebook, in which she'd jotted down the information he needed. "I asked all your questions."

The PI nodded. "Thanks."

"You're welcome. Lori also told me she saw a photo of the man who Bri met in Mexico." Tara's attention turned to Matt. "She said he wasn't you. The man in the picture had darker blond hair, and he was only about five ten. And you're over six feet."

Matt nodded. "Six two."

"My sister was my height, five eight. Lori said that the guy in the photo was only a few inches taller than Bri."

Matt looked concerned. "You okay?"

"I just wish I could find the picture," she said, unable to keep the frustration out of her voice. "Then we might discover who this guy is. I'm sorry."

He brushed a strand of hair from her face. "Why are you sorry?"

She felt tears building again. "I wanted to help you."

His coffee eyes were filled with tenderness. "Oh, Tara, you have helped me. You've brought me closer than ever before."

Jim spoke. "We are getting closer. This Cathy Pennington was in the address book."

"Wasn't her phone number disconnected?" Matt asked.

"Yeah, but according to Lori she's married to a Marine." Jim grinned. "I can trace a military man."

"When you find her, I'd like to talk with Cathy, too," Tara said.

Matt nodded. "Definitely. We're in this together."

Matt pulled his car into the driveway just after nine o'clock that evening. Their flight had been delayed, so they had a quiet dinner at the airport. Sloan had headed to San Diego to check out new leads.

Matt watched Tara get out of the car. He knew she was troubled by the day's events. It must have hurt her to know her sister had a life that she knew nothing about. And he knew she felt guilty she hadn't been there to help Bri when she got into trouble.

Matt came around the car and took her hand. "Come on, let's go for a walk."

She resisted at first, then allowed him to lead her across the yard. Together they walked down the dozen steps to the deserted beach.

For the first few minutes they walked with only the sound of the surf to fill the silence between them. Matt knew there was a lot of pain locked inside Tara, but in time he hoped she would be able to deal with it all.

He guided Tara to the sand and took a seat in front of a large piece of driftwood, made a place for her between his legs and drew her back against his chest. "You can't blame yourself for what happened to your sister."

Tara didn't say anything.

"Bri chose her life. You chose yours."

Looking over her shoulder, she glared at him. "You don't know why Bri left Phoenix—why she left me."

"Come on, Tara. Stop beating yourself up over this. Bri had the same life you did, the same chances."

"You don't understand," she argued. "Bri needed more. She needed love from our father. A father who was never around."

"What about you, Tara? Was your father around to love you?"

She glanced at the surf and shrugged. "I didn't need him as much as Bri. I could handle his rejection, but Bri couldn't." The hurt was evident in her voice. "She was always running after men. All she ever wanted was love."

He cupped her chin and turned her toward him. The moonlight illuminated the tears on her face. Matt couldn't stand to see her pain. "We all need love, Tara. You're no exception. Everyone needs to be touched...held." He leaned forward and touched her tempting lips with his. She sucked in a breath. "Or kissed." He returned to her mouth. This time there wasn't any doubt of his hunger.

Matt couldn't stop himself. He'd never wanted a woman like he wanted Tara McNeal. Sooner or later he was going to have to give her up, but he'd hold on to her now as if his life depended on it. Maybe it did. It had been so long since he'd allowed himself any physical contact with a woman. He was starved. One sexy redhead had him hungry with the overwhelming need to taste her.

He tightened his hold on her and could feel her tremble. Or was it him trembling? He didn't know. He knew only that he never wanted to let her go. And Tara's eagerness matched his as he delved into her mouth, his tongue dancing with hers. The tiny whimpering sound she made was quickly swept away in the breeze.

Matt's hand went under her sweater to her warm skin, then her breasts. Cupping the fullness, he managed to shift the lacy fabric to bare her softness. Tara clung to him as his fingers moved against the sensitive nipples, causing them to harden against his palm.

He hugged her tightly, wanting to feel all of her. "Have you any idea what you're doing to me?"

In the moonlight he could see her eyes shimmering. "Oh, Matt."

The sound of his name on her lips nearly sent him over the edge. He kissed her again, his body aching to make love to her right there on the beach. It was crazy, but Tara McNeal had him so off balance he couldn't think straight.

Suddenly she struggled and pushed at him to release her. "We have to stop. I need to go inside," she said.

Knowing she was right, he nodded and helped her up. By the time they were at the house, he still couldn't let her go. He pulled her into his arms and let his kisses relay what he wanted, needed. Her.

Tara ended the kiss. "Matt, this isn't a good idea. We have to stop or..."

He looked at her, her eyes mirroring his desire. "Would that be so bad?"

She glanced away, but Matt refused to let her deny her feelings. "Tell me you don't want me, Tara, and I'll walk away."

Matt refused to let his common sense interfere with his desire for her. So he wasn't going to think at all. He just wanted Tara McNeal, hot and willing in his bed. But when he pushed open the door to the house, the sound of a baby's cry quickly brought him back to reality.

Tara came out of her daze and rushed into the bedroom. She found Juanita pacing the floor with Erin.

"Oh, good, you're back," the housekeeper said.

"What's wrong," Tara asked as she took the baby from Juanita.

"Erin's been a little fussy since she woke up from her nap. She didn't finish her bottle. She felt warm, but I took her temperature three times, and it's just a little over normal."

"What's the matter, sweetie?" Tara crooned, trying to conceal her panic. "You got a tummy ache?"

The four-month-old began to scream in earnest.

Tara looked at Matt for help.

Matt immediately took charge. "Juanita, will you get my bag in the study?" He laid the baby on the bed and stripped her down to her diaper.

"What do you think is wrong?" Tara stood beside him, letting Erin know she was close.

"Too soon to tell, yet," he said. "But I'll find out."

The housekeeper returned with the bag and Matt took out his stethoscope and began his examination. He checked the baby's ears, throat and mouth. Everything he did only seemed to make Erin more unhappy.

He pulled off his stethoscope. "Juanita, do you have any of the medicine you used on your granddaughter's sore gums?"

She nodded. "Yes, it's in my bathroom. I'll get it." The woman was gone and back in no time.

Matt checked the label, then removed the cap, put a small amount on the tip of his finger and began to rub it on Erin's lower gum. Slowly the child's cries subsided, and she began to make a sucking noise.

"Does that feel better?" Matt smiled at the baby.

"Poor *niña*," Juanita said. "I didn't see any teeth coming in."

"There isn't a tooth, but her gums look a little swollen. I just guessed that might be the problem."

Tara was amazed. "Isn't Erin a little young to get teeth? The book said—"

"Kids don't always follow the book," Matt said as he leaned over the baby. "But it would be nice, princess, if we knew all the rules, wouldn't it?" To Tara's surprise Erin grinned at him.

Juanita sighed. "Well, you three can continue the party, I'm going to bed." She started out the door.

Tara raced to catch up with her. "Juanita, thank you so much for watching her today. I wouldn't have gone if I'd known this would happen."

"It wasn't a problem. I love that little girl. I was just worried I had done something wrong." She glanced at Matt. "It's nice having a doctor around."

"Yes, it is," Tara admitted, then realized that only moments ago, she'd nearly stepped over the line with that doctor.

"I hope your trip was worth it," Juanita said.

"I'll tell you all about it in the morning." Tara hugged the woman. "You get some sleep."

Tara went back to the bed where Matt was playing with Erin. "I can handle her now. So you can go to bed."

They exchanged a long glance, and she realized she still wanted him. But it was impossible. They'd nearly made a mistake tonight. "About earlier..." The words caught in her throat. She didn't know exactly what to say.

He moved around the bed and held her shoulders. "Look, Tara. Today was an emotional day. We both got carried away by the moment. I don't want you to have any regrets.''

*Oh, there will be no regrets,* she thought. A night in Matt Landers's arms would be a dream. Too bad she would eventually have to wake up.

During the next week, Matt kept his distance from Tara. Not that he didn't want to be around her, but he knew she was at a vulnerable place right now. Besides, he didn't need the temptation. *Don't get involved,* he told himself. She and Erin would be leaving before summer's end. But right now, he was in misery, having her across the hall.

Tonight, like most nights, he lay in his king-size bed, his hands behind his head, listening for Erin's cry. Then he heard her. He glanced at his bedside clock. It was twelve-thirty.

He heard Tara getting out of bed. Smiling, he could picture her hair mussed from sleep, her warm body adorned by that silly oversize T-shirt she wore. She couldn't look any sexier if she were wrapped in satin.

His attention was drawn to the sound of her voice. Her tone was hushed and soft. He closed his eyes and imagined her whispering to him, telling him to touch her, caress her. Soon his body was hard and aching. If only Tara would enter his room, climb into his bed…

Damn. He had to stop wanting what he couldn't have. Even getting the DNA test back today told him what he already knew, but it seemed to finalize the last threat, the last connection to Erin…and Tara. Sitting up, he raked his fingers through his hair. Why couldn't he be satisfied with his life, his career? He'd resigned himself long ago to the fact he wasn't cut out for someone like Tara. Someone who wanted a family.

Besides, there were plenty of women out there who wanted him. And with no commitment. He made a mental note to call a few of them. The charity ball was coming up. That would be a great time to get back in the social scene.

He stood and put on his robe. In time, his life would get back to normal. Could he handle the wait? He pulled open his door and walked down the hall to the kitchen. He poured himself a glass of milk and quickly downed it. After rinsing the glass in the sink, he turned and found Tara standing in the doorway.

"Matt." She looked as surprised as he did.

"Hi, Tara," he managed to say as his eyes took in that damn sexy T-shirt. "Finish Erin's feeding?"

She held up the empty bottle. "Yeah. I haven't figured out how to get her to sleep all night, though."

"Try giving her a bottle about ten-thirty, and I bet she'll sleep through."

Tara smiled. "Hey, I'll try anything to get an uninterrupted night's sleep."

*Something you wouldn't have if you were in my bed,* he thought. "Try it." He started out of the kitchen, but she stopped him.

"Matt, have you heard anything from Jim?"

She was standing so close he caught her intoxicating scent. His body came alive. God help him. "No, he's still trying to get through the military red tape."

"Well, at least Erin and I are moving to the cottage tomorrow so you'll have your house back." Her eyes met his, mirroring the want and desire he felt every time she was near. "I...I know it's been an inconvenience for you."

Hell, she'd been more than that. She'd been driving him crazy. He couldn't seem to help himself when he reached for her and pulled her against him. He paused, but when she didn't resist, he bent his head and kissed her. Kissed her with all the pent-up feeling he'd held in check all week.

She clung to him while the fire between them raged. His pulse raced. His body burned for her. But he couldn't have her. Slowly he broke off the kiss. Even hearing her whimper of protest, he managed to back away.

"I'm sorry, that shouldn't have happened."

She nodded. "You're right. I mean...I'm only here temporarily. I have my teaching job, and you have your career...."

"That's all I have room for in my life," he added.

Tara tried to act brave. She'd never been in this kind of situation. If Matt knew how inexperienced she really was, he would probably laugh.

"I wasn't asking you for anything, Matt," she said. "But we seem to have this problem of keeping our hands off each other."

She stared at his bare chest, aching to touch his heated skin. Before she realized what was happening, he had her pinned against the wall, his mouth devouring hers.

His hands roamed down her sides, tugging at the hem of her nightshirt. He reached around and cupped her bottom, pulling her closer. When she felt the hot weight of his arousal burning against her stomach, she groaned and instinctively pressed into him.

He trailed kisses over her face, down her neck.

Then he began to raise her shirt, exposing her panties. "I'm only human, Tara, and so close to the edge," he whispered, tugging the material higher. Inch by inch he revealed her skin along with the desire in his eyes.

A sound came from Juanita's room.

Matt dropped her shirt and drew her protectively in his arms until the noise faded and all they could hear was their labored breathing. Matt closed his eyes as if he were trying to regain control. Then finally he stood back. "I'm sorry, Tara. I know I keep telling you that, but I mean it. I have no business taking advantage of you."

Disappointment rushed through her. "You're not taking advantage."

"Help me here, Tara." He raked his fingers through his hair. "I'm trying damn hard to do the right thing. So please, just go back to bed…alone, then tomorrow you won't have any regrets."

Tara didn't wait for any more instructions. She did as he asked and hurried down the hall, knowing in her heart she could never regret making love with Matt.

But she also knew there would be nothing more.

Two days later, Tara was reading a story to her group of five-and six-year-olds when she glanced up and saw Matt coming into the nursery. What was he doing at the day-care center?

After getting her group settled for lunch, she wandered into the glass-enclosed nursery to find Matt holding Erin. They were both giggling as he lifted her high in the air. Then he turned and locked eyes with Tara.

She hadn't seen him since the night in the kitchen. He looked wonderful, but tired.

"Hi." He cradled the baby against his large chest. "How are things going?"

"Good. It's a lot of work, but the kids are great." She brushed her hair from her face and bit her lower lip, realizing she hadn't put on any makeup. "I guess you've been busy, too."

"Yes, I had surgery this morning and complications with two patients in ICU."

"What brings you by here?"

"I wanted to see how Erin was doing with her new tooth." He glanced at the small bandage on Tara's hand. "And I heard from Dr. Meyers that he removed your stitches."

She nodded and raised her hand to show the gauze wrapped around her thumb. "I might have a little scar, but not bad."

"Good." He glanced around the nursery. "Tara, do you think you can take some time for lunch? I spoke with Jim this morning."

"I...I probably can. Sure, I'll go ask Charlene."

"Okay, I'll meet you outside then."

Tara took Erin from him and put her in the crib, left instructions with her co-worker, Emily, then went to the director and asked for a break. She met Matt in the corridor and they walked to the cafeteria. Seated at a table, Tara felt like a teenager. She was having difficulty looking directly at Matt. He was a beautiful man. Today, he wore a camel-colored fitted shirt with a paisley tie and pleated cocoa-brown trousers.

Suddenly Matt's gaze captured hers, and Tara's heart began to pound. She glanced away, wondering if he'd been thinking about what happened between them just a few days ago...how close they'd come to making love.

"How's everything at the cottage?" he asked her. "Any leaks?"

"Fine. You can't tell there was ever a tree branch over the bed," she joked. "And since it hasn't rained, I can't tell about the leaks."

He gave her one of those smiles that took her breath away. "I guess I could turn on the hose and squirt the roof."

They both laughed.

Matt felt ridiculous. He knew Tara was as uncomfortable as he was. Hell, that was why he'd been avoiding her, or he'd chance the temptation. She didn't need that. But she was hard to resist.

"You said Jim called you."

Her voice interrupted his thoughts. "Oh, yes, he phoned this morning. He found Cathy Guthrie Pennington. She lives off base in San Diego with her husband, Sergeant Robert Pennington. A neighbor told him they're away on vacation to see his parents and will return next week."

Tara sighed. "Oh, I hope she'll be able to tell us something."

"I'm counting on it," he said. "Cathy is probably the only other person who's met this imposter."

"Maybe Bri sent her a picture or something that will help us."

Matt was hopeful and optimistic. "We have to follow through on all leads. It's crucial we catch the man. This maniac has applied for another credit card in my name. And he's leased *another* car. I just hope the police can track him down by the automobile plates.''

"Oh, Matt, I'm sorry." Tara laid her hand on his. He immediately felt her warmth, and his body stirred to life.

"It's not your fault. But I've got to get this guy before he destroys what's left of my life—my career."

"You will," Tara said, her voice soothing. "May I go with you to talk with Cathy?"

"Hey, aren't you that famous doctor?"

Matt looked up to see Cari coming toward the table. The gleam in her eyes told him she hadn't missed the cozy scene. He stood and greeted her. "Cari, I didn't know you were working today."

Cari Malone sat in the empty chair. "I'm not, just some finishing touches for the charity ball." She turned to Tara. "Hi, Tara, I hope you're coming, too." Her head swiveled to Matt. "You did invite her, didn't you?"

"I…I hadn't thought about it." Matt found himself stumbling over his words. "Come on, Cari. It's boring as hell."

The blonde looked insulted. "I beg your pardon, Dr. Landers. I worked hard to make the evening enjoyable. So Tara, I'm personally inviting you."

"But…I can't. I mean…I wouldn't know anyone. Besides, I have nothing to wear."

"You'll know plenty of people by the time the evening is in full swing. And as for clothes, I have plenty of dresses." She waved her hand. "I'm sure we can find something for you. Come by the house tonight." Her blue eyes lit up. "We'll barbecue. Then the guys can handle the kids while we go upstairs and find something that will dazzle every man in the place. See you about seven.''

Before either of them could say a word, Cari rushed out.

Tara finally looked at Matt. ''Look, I don't need to go. I know Cari just invited me because I'm staying at the cottage. I don't want you to feel as if you have to take me. I mean, you could already have a date.''

He hadn't thought about another woman since Tara McNeal walked into his office. ''No, I don't have a date. And I'm sorry, Tara. I should have invited you. I just think of the event as a social duty. I'm usually so busy working the crowd for research money.'' He smiled. ''I'd be honored if you'd go with me to the ball.''

## Chapter Nine

At seven o'clock, Cari greeted Tara, Erin and Matt at the front door of the large Malone home.

"So you made it," she said, then moved aside and motioned for them both to enter.

Tara held back a gasp as she stepped into the huge entry. The marble floor gleamed as she walked across the room to a circular staircase. Suddenly there was a ruckus, and the oldest Malone child, Danny, came racing down the steps. He was followed by a darling girl of about four with a blond ponytail.

"You're 'pose to wait for me, Danny," she shouted, then came to a quick halt at the bottom of the steps when she saw the guests. "Sorry, Mom. I didn't mean to yell."

Cari gave her daughter a stern look. "Tara, this is our daughter, Krissy. Krissy, this is Tara and her little girl, Erin."

"Hi, I'm going to be five years old. Can I hold your baby?"

Matt swept the girl up in his arms and kissed both her cheeks. "How about later, squirt, when you're sitting in a chair?"

"'Kay." She wrapped her arms around his neck and kissed him. Then she examined Tara. "You're pretty. Are you Dr. Matt's woman?"

Several throats were cleared as heat rushed to Tara's cheeks.

Cari gasped. "Kristin Eleanor Malone, what did I tell you about asking so many questions?"

The cute child rested her head on Matt's shoulder. "It's not polite. Sorry, Mom."

"Just watch it from now on," Cari warned. "Now, where is your father?"

"He's changing Matthew's diaper."

Commotion upstairs alerted them to the rest of the Malone family joining them. Tara looked up to see Nick Malone carrying his toddler son, a stocky, dark-haired boy, down the steps. "Hey, don't start the party without us," Nick said.

"We wouldn't think of it," Cari said. "You're in charge of the grill."

"Good, it's our night to cook, right, guys?" Nick said as he set his son down. The boy grinned as he pointed to Matt. "Matt," he cried and took a few awkward steps across the floor.

Matt crouched and released Krissy in time to catch the boy in his arms. "Well, aren't you a big boy."

"Big boy," Matthew repeated proudly.

Everyone laughed.

"Well, Tara," Nick said, "you've met all the family, but there's still time to run for the hills."

"I wouldn't think of it," she assured him. "You are very lucky to have such a beautiful family."

Nick pulled his wife into a loving embrace. "That's something you don't have to tell me. I count my blessings every day." He kissed his wife.

There were a few seconds of awkwardness, then Danny spoke. "They do this all the time."

Matt put his arm around Danny's shoulder. "Just give yourself a few years and you won't think it's so bad."

"Danny already has a girlfriend," Krissy announced. "He talks to her on the phone. I heard them."

Danny's face reddened in anger. "You better just stay out of my room, you little…"

"Danny," his father said with a warning look.

"Dad, she's always bugging me."

"We'll discuss it later."

"Yes, later," Cari agreed. "Let's go out back to the patio."

They walked through the house, and once again Tara was amazed at the beautifully decorated rooms. And once outside on the patio, she looked across a huge backyard. The pool was fenced in, probably for the safety of the kids, but the grassy area had plenty of space for a jungle gym and several riding toys to keep the kids occupied.

"Isn't it a shame our kids are so deprived?" Cari said.

What fascinated Tara the most was that the children had everything to play with, but all fought for Matt's attention. And he truly seemed to enjoy being with them, too.

After a dinner of steak for the adults and hamburgers for the kids, Cari told the men to clear up, then she took Tara by the hand and they went upstairs to the large master suite.

Done in shades of blues and plums, the room had plush cream-colored carpet and floral print wallpaper that matched the comforter on the king-size bed. A window seat overlooked the backyard, and candles lined every ledge and furniture top.

"This is a beautiful room," Tara said.

Cari smiled. "Thanks. I redecorated after Matthew was born. Nick's contribution was the candles." She blushed. "They have a special meaning for us."

Tara was surprised to realize that she truly envied the woman the loving relationship she shared with her husband. For the first time, Tara understood what it was like to love a man. She froze. She loved Matt. Her heart began to race. Oh, God! For the first time in her life she was head-over-heels in love.

But why Dr. Matt Landers, a man who'd buried himself in his career? She doubted he was capable of returning her love.

"Come on," Cari said, walking to the large closet and pulling open the double doors, exposing a row of dresses. "We have our work cut out for us."

Suddenly Tara felt out of place. She'd never gone to a prom, never even tried on an evening dress.

"Don't look so frightened. This is going to be fun." Cari rubbed her hands together. "More importantly, you're going to make the evening fun for Matt. He doesn't take much time for a social life. And I've been praying for years for him to find someone like you."

"Me?" Tara shook her head in denial. "You don't even know me. I'm nothing to Matt."

Cari smiled. "I know better. You loved your sister, and you love your niece enough to put off your own life to search for her father." She walked to Tara. "Just make sure you take some time for yourself."

"My first concern is Erin."

"Of course, but there's also room for a special man. Matt."

Tara felt the heat rush to her face. "But he doesn't think of me that way."

Cari looked unconvinced. "A person would have to be blind not to see how he looks at you. The man is definitely interested. More than he realizes, and probably more than you realize. So," she sighed, "let's make it so he can't resist you." Cari took Tara's hand and together they went into the closet. "I think you'd look stunning in black," she announced. "And I have a dress that can work magic. I know from personal experience."

Cari dug through the plastic-covered dresses and pulled out a strapless black gown. Tara swallowed hard, wandering what she'd gotten herself into.

Matt tugged at his bow tie for the hundredth time. Then he checked his watch. It was nearly six, and they needed to meet Cari and Nick by six-thirty. He brushed the wrinkles from his tuxedo pants and wished he'd never agreed to this.

He'd heard the talking in the guest room Juanita and Tara had disappeared into two hours ago. It couldn't possibly take this long to get dressed, could it?

Something caught his attention. He glanced up and saw Tara coming down the hall. His mouth grew dry. She was dressed in a strapless black gown that showed off her delicate shoulders and full breasts, giving her just a hint of cleavage. He lowered his gaze to the slightly gathered waistline, but it was the slit that revealed one long leg that had his body temperature rising. When she walked across the room, he saw the strappy, heeled sandals adorning her slender feet.

"Do I look okay?" she asked timidly.

"Huh?" He jerked his gaze to her auburn hair, which had been pulled back from her face with tiny sparkling ornaments buried in her short curls.

"Do I look okay?" she asked again.

She was incredibly beautiful, his racing pulse was evidence of that. "You look nice."

"Nice!" Juanita came out carrying Erin. "I'm going to get you an appointment to get your eyes checked. Tara looks beautiful. She'll be the belle of the ball."

Matt smiled. "That's what I meant."

"Then say what you mean," Juanita chided.

Matt didn't need a lecture about dating etiquette. "Then give me a chance," he murmured as he walked by his housekeeper, reached for a flower on the table and went to Tara. "Here, this is for the lovely lady."

Tara smiled. "Oh, thank you, Matt."

Matt glanced at Juanita to see her pleased smile. "We'd better be going."

Tara nodded and kissed Erin goodbye. She promised Juanita they wouldn't be late.

"Don't worry," Juanita replied. "Erin is staying here with me tonight."

Matt took Tara by the arm, and they started out the door to the car. He inhaled the soft scent of her perfume and knew that only a miracle would help him keep his promise. His promise to keep his distance from Tara McNeal. Impossible.

The ballroom at the four-star hotel had been decorated with thousands of flowers and twinkling lights. White linen and silver covered the round tables, and there were engraved placards at every seat. A band played softly as the town's wealthy, men dressed in tuxedos and women in ball gowns, chatted with one another.

And there stood Tara, not knowing a soul and suddenly having several second thoughts about coming tonight. This was so far from her world.

Then Matt appeared at her side. "Sorry, Tara. I got cornered by Mrs. Petty. I wouldn't have stayed and talked, but she's been a big contributor to the cardiac unit."

Tara couldn't help staring at her handsome date. Dr. Matt Landers in a tux was a lethal combination. And he was hers…for the night.

"You don't have to apologize. I know you're busy, and the hospital needs the donations. I wish there was something I could do to help. Maybe Cari needs me." She started to walk off, but Matt took her by the arm, holding her close.

"Oh, no, you don't. You're my date, and far too beautiful to let run around loose," he said. "Besides, if you're going to help anyone, it will be me. At the auction."

She loved his possessiveness. "Oh, Matt. I'm not really good in front of people."

He frowned and touched her cheek, sending shivers through her. "That's not true, Tara. I've seen you

handle the kids at the center with ease. You're perfect.''

She was too weak to argue and allowed Matt to
take her by the hand and together they circled the
room, mingling with people.

It wasn't so bad, Tara thought when they sat down
for dinner with a nice older couple, who had talked
about their grandchildren and Erin. Bless Cari for
arranging the seating.

Then came time for the silent auction. Matt
worked in front of the podium just as well as he did
everything else. Perfectly. Tara was mesmerized.
And she wasn't the only one. He charmed the ladies,
and the men didn't know what hit them. He also
fussed over every donated prize Tara held up for bid.
Surprisingly, she found she was having fun, too.

Finally the auction came to an end with an over-
the-top amount of money collected for Riverhaven.
With the business over, the dancing began. Nick and
Cari invited Matt and her to join them.

''Unless you want to go home,'' Matt said.

Tara shrugged. ''What about Erin?''

''She's asleep,'' Matt said. ''So what other excuse
do you have?''

''I can't dance very well,'' she said.

''Neither do I.'' He winked. ''We'll just move
around blindly together, and hopefully the dance police won't make us leave.''

That made her laugh.

Matt knew he should take Tara home, but something made him lead her out to the floor. All he could
think about was holding her in his arms, feeling her
softness pressed to him. He placed his chin against

her hair and bit back a groan as she moved against him.

"It's been a lovely evening. Thank you for bringing me." Tara raised her head and flashed her emerald eyes at him.

"You made it pretty special for me, Tara," Matt said and pulled her into his arms.

He tightened his hold and moved his leg between hers, immediately causing friction. He had to be insane, but he placed her hand against his chest and wrapped his other arm around her back. Their dance steps began to slow. They were doing nothing more than shifting back and forth, his body hot and aching from her sizzling touch.

Dear Lord help him, he was about to explode. What made him think he could stay away from her, stop wanting her? He drew back and looked at Tara, seeing the longing in her eyes.

"Do you want to leave?" he asked, unable to keep the hoarseness out of his voice.

At her nod, he gripped her hand and they headed to the table. He grabbed Tara's purse and said a quick goodbye to the Malones. But not before he caught Nick's wink and Cari's knowing smile. Hell, he didn't care. All he had on his mind was Tara.

They made it to the parking lot and into the car. His first mistake was looking at her, at her inviting mouth. He couldn't stop himself. He reached across the car and pulled her toward him. His head lowered, and he crushed his lips against hers. She answered with eagerness and opened her mouth, allowing him to sip at her sweetness, but it wasn't enough.

He broke off the kiss and made her look at him. "I want you, Tara. And when I get you home, I'm going to show you just how much. But if you don't want the same thing, tell me now.''

"Take me home, Matt," she whispered.

Her whispered words made him smile. ''Whatever the lady wants.'' He quickly strapped her in the safety belt and started the car.

At the house, Matt climbed out and hurried around the car to help her out. As soon as she was standing, he drew her into his arms and kissed her again. They were both breathless when he released her, then pulled her into the house. Careful not to wake anyone, they tiptoed down the hall, only stopping to check on Erin. Seeing the baby was sound asleep, Matt tugged on Tara's hand and led her into his dimly lit bedroom. After the door closed, he backed her against it and went to work on her mouth again.

One kiss led to another as he stripped off his jacket. Tara helped with his tie, studs, then his shirt, and by the time he was bare chested, he had to fight for control.

''Now you,'' he said, and placed a soft kiss against her already swollen lips.

Tara wasn't going to fight her attraction for Matt any longer. She wanted him, if only for one night, and she wanted to experience what it would be like to love this man. To pretend he loved her.

She turned, giving him access to the zipper off her dress. He leaned over, pressed a kiss against the sensitive skin along her neck and every nerve in her body leaped at his touch. The zipper finally gave way, and he helped her step out of the gown. He lay the black satin on a chair in the corner, then turned to her.

Tara shivered as his gaze raked over her nearly

nude body. The dress hadn't needed a bra, and she wore only a pair of lacy bikini pants and thigh-high sheer stockings Cari had talked her into buying. Now she was glad she did.

"Oh, God! If I'd known what you were wearing under the dress, I doubt if I could have made it through the evening."

He drew her against him as blood surged through her body. "Anyone ever tell you how damn sexy you look in black?" he growled against her neck.

"No, no one. Show me how sexy," she said boldly.

"Oh, I plan to, but this is going to take awhile," he promised.

Tara's breath caught at his words. She hoped that her inexperience wouldn't turn him off. But she didn't have a chance to think. Matt swung her into his arms and carried her across the room. He set her down next to his king-size bed, stepped back and kicked off his shoes, then he unfastened his trousers and let them slip to the floor along with his briefs, leaving him totally and beautifully nude. Tara was so fascinated all she could think about was his incredible body.

Then he tossed back the bedcovers and laid her down.

He pulled off her shoes and slowly began removing her stockings, then her panties. "You know the past weeks, I thought I'd go crazy from wanting you." A thrill raced through her as his gaze combed over her body.

"You have me now," she said, trying to keep the trembling out of her voice. "Oh, Matt. Make love to me." Reaching up, she pulled Matt to her as her mouth sought his in a hungry kiss. No way was she going to let him change his mind.

He tore away, only to trail more kisses down her neck until his mouth closed over her breast. He drew deeply on her nipple, and she gasped at the sudden pleasure. He continued to tease the bud until it grew hard against his tongue, then paid homage to the other.

Then his mouth roamed lower over her stomach, and she gripped the sheets, feeling the shivers of delight everywhere. He moved lower, using his tongue to drive her over the edge. Within moments she began to fall, then she saw stars as her body shook and she cried out in release.

Matt was there with her, holding her until she calmed. "You are so beautiful," he said, his voice husky.

Tara could barely speak as she stroked his jaw, then kissed him. It didn't take long for the heat to build between them. She burned to pleasure Matt. She forgot her shyness and her inexperience as her hands quickly became busy. She raked her fingers over his chest, tracing his solid muscle and broad shoulders. Bravely, she leaned forward and kissed his flat nipple. He responded with a throaty groan. All at once Tara found she was pressed into the mattress as Matt's body covered hers. His mouth closed over hers, his tongue delving inside, mating with hers.

He broke off, breathing hard. "Ah, Tara. You're making me crazy. I can't wait." His hand went between their bodies and tested to see if she was ready. Her wetness only aroused him more.

"Please, Matt. Make love to me—now." She raised her hips in invitation and immediately felt him press against her, then there was the wonderful pressure as he pushed into her.

As he whispered her name, their bodies came together and the pace quickened. Tara gasped as the sensation nearly drove her off the bed. She bit her lip, wondering if she could die from the pleasure. Clinging to him, she wrapped her legs around his back as he drove into her, each stroke bringing her closer and closer to heaven.

Matt raised himself up. He looked so beautiful. She had to bite back the words, ''I love you.'' Suddenly she felt something coiling inside, then with Matt's encouraging words, a spasm took her, and she began to tumble over and over again through space.

Even before she could recover, she heard Matt groan her name, then he collapsed on top of her. Tara held onto him tightly, trying to hold firmly to the feelings, not wanting anything to intrude on their perfect night.

Matt moved next to her, tucking her close to his side. ''You okay?'' he asked.

She smiled. ''I think if I felt any better I'd die.''

He kissed the top of her head. ''That wouldn't do any good for my reputation as a doctor.''

She turned her head to him. ''I guess you could revive me.''

''It would be my pleasure, Ms. McNeal.'' His fingers caressed her arm, then he pulled her closer as her breasts brushed against his chest. Finally he brought her on top of him, unable to stop the need to mesh her body with his again. ''I have plans for the rest of the evening,'' he said.

Matt tried not to think about the feelings Tara McNeal stirred in him. For years he'd been in control of his body and his emotions. That had all changed tonight. Hell, he'd even forgotten about protection. Not that Tara had any worries about pregnancy. He shut his eyes as a sadness he'd never known before filled him.

Then Tara shifted against him with a soft sigh. Again his body began to respond, and he tightened his hold on her. No, he wasn't going to ruin it, and he wasn't going to think of what he couldn't have. When the time came he would have to find a way to send Tara away. Just not tonight.

Matt blinked and squinted in the sun's glare through the bedroom window. He rolled over on the mattress, and certain parts of his body rebelled, bringing back memories of last night and the times they'd made love.

His eyes shot open, and he realized he was alone. Tara was gone. The clock on the bedside table read ten-fifteen.

"Damn, I never sleep this late." Raking a hand through his hair, he glanced around the room. Where was Tara?

He climbed out of bed and started for the door. Then he stopped, realized he was stark naked. Hell, what was wrong with him? He knew, but didn't want to analyze what he was feeling. Not now. Not after discovering that spending the night making love to her had only increased his appetite, and not just for her body…but for all of her.

He needed to see Tara. But not before he cleared the fog from his head and washed her intoxicating scent from his body. Matt headed for the shower.

Twenty minutes later he walked into the kitchen to find Juanita—alone.

"Morning," he murmured as he went to the coffeemaker and poured himself a cup.

"I was wondering when you were going to show your face." She gave him the once-over. "Must have been quite a party."

Matt could feel the heat creep up his neck. "Who...told you about the party?"

"Well, Tara, of course. She was feeding Erin breakfast about seven when I left for church." The older woman smiled. "Tara said the ball was wonderful. She's never had such a good time." Suddenly Juanita walked over and kissed Matt on the cheek. "Bless you for taking that girl." She turned serious. "I don't think life's been easy on her."

Matt didn't know what to say. "Then I'm glad Tara had a good time. She helped me with the auction, too." *Then we came home and I seduced her,* he added silently.

Juanita busied herself making toast. "Good, she was so afraid she wouldn't fit in with those people. I told her that people are all alike, some good, some bad."

"She seemed to fit in better than I did."

"Tara said you stayed and danced." She went to the refrigerator and took out some jam, and Matt wondered how much the two had talked about. "I would have liked to have seen that. I bet you two made a handsome couple."

Seeing the challenging look on Juanita's face, Matt wasn't about to argue. Nor did he want to. "Where's Tara this morning?"

"She's at the cottage. Said she only slept in the

guest room last night because she didn't want to wake Erin.''

Not making eye contact with Juanita, Matt took a seat at the table. ''Yes, it was rather late when we got home.''

Juanita set the plate of toast in front of him. ''Well, whatever time you got in, you made Tara a very happy woman.''

Tara put Erin down for her nap. Poor baby, she was exhausted from all their playing this morning. Tara had probably enjoyed it even more than her niece. It had seemed like ages since they'd shared any time together. Tara stroked the baby's cheek. How much she had changed over the past few weeks. Not only had her four-month-old niece acquired a tooth, but she was holding up her head, even rolling over onto her stomach. By the time they got home, Mrs. Lynch wouldn't even know her.

Home. Phoenix seemed like another lifetime, especially after last night. Tara's face suddenly heated up, recalling details of their lovemaking.

Oh, Lord. How could she act so... What? Wanton? Never in her life had she shared such intimacy with a man. And Matt had been so tender, so loving with her.

But Tara knew it wasn't realistic to think that anything could come of it. It was one night, and Matt had never offered her more. She'd gone into his bed without any promises. But that hadn't stopped her from falling in love with the man.

There was a soft knock on the door, and Tara could see Matt standing on the stoop. She took a breath for strength and hurried to answer it.

"Good morning," she said with a cheery smile. But one look at the man dressed in khaki shorts and a white T-shirt set her pulse racing.

"Morning, Tara. How are you?" He stepped inside.

"I'm fine."

He glanced around, then looked at her. She could see that he was as awkward as she was about what had happened between them. Oh, God. Please don't let him be sorry.

"I'm sorry I fell asleep... I didn't know you left...."

She shrugged. How did one handle the morning after? "It's okay, Erin woke up and I didn't want Juanita to come for her and find... Then she would have known...."

He smiled, then he took a step closer and drew her into his arms. "God, you're beautiful this morning," he breathed as his mouth came down on hers. A whimper came from her throat, and wrapping her arms around his back, she pressed herself against him, and a thousand sparks shot off around her.

Finally he released her and took a step back. "I've wanted to do that since I woke up this morning, alone."

"I didn't want to leave you," she said, breathless. "I wanted to curl up against your warm body...."

"Stop," he groaned, then took another step back from her. "There's no doubt that I want you, Tara. Even though I know it's wrong...."

Dread overtook her. Was he regretting last night?

The phone rang, bringing them both back to reality. Tara hurried to answer it. "Hello," she said.

"Tara, it's Juanita. I'm sorry to bother you, but I need to talk to Matt."

"Just a minute." She handed Matt the phone.

"Yes, Juanita?" He frowned as he listened, then said, "I'll be there in a few minutes. Have Mr. Douglas wait for me in the study."

Matt hung up, wondering what could be so important that it brought the hospital administrator here on a Sunday.

"Sorry, I've got to go back to the house. Harry Douglas is waiting to see me." He went to her. His hand stroked her soft cheek, every part of him aching to drag her into his arms and kiss away all the doubt he saw in her eyes.

Instead he dropped his hand and said, "We need to talk about what's happening...between us. Why don't I meet you on the beach steps in about thirty minutes?"

She nodded hesitantly.

"Good, I'll be back," he promised, then hurried out the door and walked to the house. He took the direct route to his office through the patio doors. He found Harry Douglas examining the antique golf clubs mounted on the wall.

Damn! Why couldn't he have one day off? The last thing he had on his mind today was hospital business. Tara lying naked on his bed flashed through his head, and he quickly shook away the picture.

Harry Douglas turned and nodded. "Hello, Matt."

"Harry," he said as he walked to his desk. "Can't I have my Sunday off?"

"If it wasn't important, I wouldn't be here," Douglas said. "But there were some things that were brought to my attention last night. This morning I called an emergency meeting of the hospital board.''

''Well, I take it you're here to tell me about it.'' Matt crossed his arms over his chest and leaned a hip on the corner of the desk. ''So let's get this over with. I have plans today.''

The older man looked troubled. ''Okay. At the ball last night, I was talking with Wolford Ivers. As you know, for years the Ivers family has been a big contributor to the hospital.''

''Yes, I talked with the Iverses last night, too.''

''Then you know that their family is in banking.''

''He's made money in a lot of things. Harry, what does this have to do with me?''

''Mr. Ivers asked several questions about your financial problems.''

Not the same old thing again. ''Did you explain what happened?''

''Yes, of course, but you have to understand, Matt, that as of now there's still a black mark on your name.''

''Which I've been trying to clear up for the past year.''

''With little success,'' Harry added. ''Matt, I spent a lot of the evening explaining your situation to several of our contributors. I made every excuse I could think of.''

Matt had had enough. ''What are you trying to say, Harry?''

''That it might be wise for the hospital, and for you, if you took some time off. Maybe go on a vacation.''

''I don't want a vacation, Harry. I'm a surgeon with patients at Riverhaven. Unless you're taking away my hospital privileges.'' Matt's heart skipped several beats. ''Are you?''

''Well, the board believes that until this matter is settled it would be best for you to take a leave of absence.'' Harry raised a hand. ''Mind you, it's just until you straighten out this mess.''

Matt cursed, feeling the crushing blow as if the man had struck him. His entire world was beginning to crumble.

''Surely, Matt, you can understand that some of the contributors are a little nervous about what's going on.''

''And I bet you didn't do a thing to ease their fears.'' Matt didn't wait for the answer. He stood. ''Fine, Harry. You say you're only doing what you have to do. Well, I'm doing what I have to do. You'll have my formal resignation on your desk in the morning.''

The man's face drained of color, and Matt thought he might have to revive him. ''Now, let's not do anything we'll regret,'' Harry said.

''The only thing I regret is that I'll be leaving my patients. Oh, I want Dr. Harper to take over my cases, and no one else. And, Harry, if any of this is leaked to the press, I might slap a lawsuit on you so fast, you won't know what hit you. And don't be surprised if the Malone donation is withdrawn. Unlike you, my friends are loyal to me.''

Harry's jaw tightened. ''Matt, can you in good conscience let that happen? The hospital depends on the Malones' generosity.''

''And how could you not stand behind your people, Harry? In fact, security was breached when my

wallet was stolen from the hospital in the first place.
I could sue you for that, too.''

''But…but.''

Matt had had enough. ''And Harry, please, don't
come to my home anymore. Any business you need
to conduct with me, you do through my lawyer.
Goodbye.''

Harry glared at him. ''This is no way to be.''

''It's exactly how I should be, Harry. You've
taken away the most important thing to me. Now, get
out.''

The man turned and marched out. Matt walked
around the desk, then dropped into a chair, feeling
his heart break into a thousand pieces. His profession
was the one thing he had in his life that gave him
purpose, and now that was gone. Everything was
gone.

## Chapter Ten

Tara waited by the steps for nearly thirty minutes. When Matt didn't show, she went looking for him. Armed with the baby monitor in case Erin woke up, Tara walked to the house. Juanita informed her that Harry Douglas had left twenty minutes ago, but Matt hadn't come out of the study.

Tara had a feeling something was wrong, and she was going to find out what it was. Entering Matt's office, she found him seated at the desk. His back was toward her as he stared out the window.

"Matt?"

He didn't turn.

She crossed the room. "You didn't come to the beach. I was worried."

"I'm fine." He sighed and wiped a hand over his face. "Why wouldn't I be fine? My life is a total disaster. I have no credit. There's a criminal out there saying he's me. I've lost thousands of dollars trying to find him." He jumped up from his chair. "Hell, now I don't even have a job."

Tara held back a gasp. "No job? How can that be? You're a wonderful surgeon."

He swung around, and she could see pain in his dark eyes. "When your reputation is in ruins, it doesn't matter how good you are." He hung his head in defeat. "I can't talk about this." He stormed out the patio door and across the lawn to the stairs leading to the beach.

Tara started after him, then changed her mind and hurried into the kitchen. "Juanita, I need a favor. Will you listen for Erin? She's napping. I have to talk to Matt. Mr. Douglas's visit upset him."

"Sure." The concerned housekeeper took the monitor. "What did that man do to him?" She waved her hand. "Never mind, you go and help him."

"I plan to." Tara crossed the lawn, but she didn't see Matt anywhere. She went down the steps and pulled off her shoes. Shielding her eyes from the sun, she glanced along the shore. In the distance she saw a runner. Matt. Tara started after him. It took a while, but she finally caught up with him about a quarter mile down the shore.

"Matt, wait," she called breathlessly.

He slowed, then stopped. He placed his hands on his hips and took several deep breaths, then turned. "I told you I didn't want to talk...."

"I just wanted to see if you're all right."

"I'm great," he retorted with cold sarcasm. "Now, go home, Tara."

"No. I'm not leaving you," she said defiantly. He

wasn't going to push her away. "What happened with Harry Douglas? Surely you're wrong about his firing you."

He shrugged as the ocean breeze ruffled his sun-streaked hair. "I didn't give him a chance. I quit."

"Oh, Matt. Why?"

"Some of the hospital contributors don't like my lousy credit rating. It seems I'm not to be trusted."

"They're wrong, Matt." Brushing her windblown hair from her face, she stepped closer. She wanted so much to go into his arms and comfort him. "You're the most trustworthy and caring man I've ever met. Anyone who really knows you, believes that."

"Harry Douglas—"

"To hell with Harry," she interrupted, shocking herself by her language. But it was worth it seeing the half smile on Matt's face.

"Why, Ms. McNeal, what a way to talk."

"I don't care." She came closer still. So close she could feel his heat, smell his wonderful scent. "You don't need Harry. You have friends who aren't going to let that weasel of a man send you away. I mean, Cari single-handedly will cause such trouble.... Oh, boy, I wouldn't want to be Harry when she finds out." Tara was drawn into the depths of his beautiful eyes. "So many people are behind you, Matt. I'm behind you."

"Don't be, Tara," he said. "I'm not the man you think I am."

"Don't try to lie to me, Matt. I've spent time with you. I know. The way you are around your pa-tients...Erin. The way you made love to me."

He groaned and looked at the water.

Tara, too, examined the waves moving against the shore, wanting the surf to drown her sadness. "Do you regret last night?" she asked.

His face was clouded with agony. "God, Tara. I could never regret making love to you. But don't try and make me some kind of martyr. I didn't even use any protection with you."

Tara's heart pounded in her chest. She hadn't thought about that. "If you're worried about me, I've…only been with one man, and that was over five years ago. And I don't think it's the right time for me to get pregnant."

His gaze held hers tenderly. "I should have protected you, Tara. I should have protected you from me." His gaze grew intense. "I can't make you any promises."

She looked at the sand. "I don't believe I asked for any."

"But you deserve more. A man…love…a family. For years, I've been dedicated to my career. There's no time for a personal life. Hell, I don't even have a career any more."

"Don't you dare say that." She gripped his arms. "You are one of the best surgeons in the country. You have to fight this, Matt."

He sighed. "I'm tired of fighting. Besides, I'm not getting anywhere looking for the man who started all this."

"You can't give up. Just weeks ago you were telling me not to. That we had to find this man—Erin's father. We will, Matt. And when we do you can go back to Riverhaven and tell them exactly what they can do with their job. Any hospital in the country will be eager to have you. So get it through your head, you're not giving up.''

Suddenly he hauled her against him. ''God, woman, I'm sure glad you're on my side.''

Tara placed her arms around Matt's neck. ''Just remember that.''

Smiling, his lips went to her ear with a soft kiss, then moved to her cheek until his mouth found hers. The wonderful sensation made Tara's knees weak as he molded her body to his.

He suddenly broke off the kiss. ''No! I can't do this.''

Hurt, Tara looked away. ''Okay, then I'll leave....''

He grabbed her arm. ''No, Tara. It's not you— never you.'' He closed his eyes. ''It's me. I can't make you any promises.''

''And I told you, you don't need to offer me anything.'' Why did she tell him this when she wanted all of this man? ''Our deal was to help each other find the imposter. It looks like you have some extra time on your hands to concentrate on finding him.''

Matt didn't want Tara to leave. Hell, after last night, he wanted her more than ever. But he was already too involved with Tara—and Erin. Each day that passed, they were becoming more important to him. A part of his life. But he knew he had to let them go...and soon. ''I want you to stay, Tara. I want your help finding this creep, for both our sakes. But we can't let last night happen again.'' Somewhere deep down inside, he was praying she would disagree. ''We can never be more than friends.''

She looked at him, her green eyes so trusting. ''That's probably for the best.''

"You're staying until school starts in August?"

She nodded.

Matt sighed in relief, but he had no idea why. He knew that Tara being in his life would be a danger.

A danger to his heart.

*What was I thinking?* Tara wondered, fighting tears.

Just hours ago, she'd agreed to help Matt continue the search. If she had any sense, she would get in her car, head home and forget she'd ever met Dr. Matthew Landers.

But she knew that would never happen. Not after she'd spent the night in his bed. Not after he'd made love to her, showed her what it felt like to be a woman. Besides, she was hopelessly in love with the man.

She walked to the crib and looked at Erin. The little girl was happily making noises at the animal mobile going around in a circle over her head. "What have I done?"

Her niece gurgled softly and kicked.

"Not only have I gone and fallen in love, but I've agreed to stay with a man who will never love me back. Totally crazy, huh?"

Erin made chatty sounds.

"I have no business thinking about a man like Matt Landers. I'm so out of his league it isn't funny. I may have gotten dressed up last night, but I'm not a satin-and-diamonds kind of girl. I'm strictly denim and cotton. But we've got to stay, sweetie. Matt needs us. And I still have that promise to your mom to keep."

The baby smiled at her.

"Just promise me, Erin, you won't let me make a fool of myself when we have to leave."

A soft knock on the door, and Tara turned to see Matt. He poked his head inside. "Hi. Mind if I come in?"

"Sure." Tara met him in the sitting area.

"I just don't want to intrude on your privacy."

Tara wished he would. She smiled. "That's funny. Here you had a woman and baby dropped on your doorstep, and you worry about their privacy."

He smiled, and Tara's pulse began to pound. He was so handsome. "I didn't want you to think that after last night you owe me...."

"If I thought that, I wouldn't be here." She felt her cheeks redden. How did one handle this kind of situation? "Didn't we decide to put that aside and move on?"

He reached for her, and she evaded him. "Look, Tara, I want to do the right thing here. I don't want to blow it again."

Just what every woman wants to hear. "If you're saying last night was a mistake—"

"No!" he said. His eyes flashed with fire. "I mean, it was wonderful, but it puts us in an awkward position."

"It doesn't have to," she said.

He started toward her, then stopped. "I just don't want you to feel obligated. I mean, I don't expect you to stay with me."

Tara's heart sank. She knew how Matt felt, but his words were crushing. "Why don't we concentrate on finding this...jerk. I wish I had a name for him."

His lips twitched. "I have several names, none of which I should say in the company of ladies."

Tara found herself laughing. "I have a feeling I know what they are."

When the laughter died, he was watching her. "I'm glad you're staying," he said, his voice husky. "And I want you to enjoy your summer, too."

She shook her head. "You don't have to worry about me. I mean, I'm working at the center and have Erin to take care of."

Suddenly the baby in question decided to make her presence known. Tara started for the crib, and Matt followed. But it was Matt who picked up the baby. "Feeling a little neglected, princess?"

Erin smiled and made a squealing sound as he blew a raspberry against her cheek. Matt shifted the baby against his arm and took Tara's hand, then walked to the sofa. They sat down, and he propped Erin against his legs. "I really came to ask you if you want to go with me to the Jewel Box tomorrow. I'm hoping to find a salesperson who might remember who bought the emerald ring."

"I thought Jim had talked with everyone."

Matt shook his head. "He's still working on leads in Mexico and L.A. Listen to me, I've spent so much time chasing this thief around, I'm talking like a professional. I'll go if you think it will help."

He looked at her. "Just your being here helps."

She felt her throat clog up. "All right."

"Then we'll plan on going about two." He kissed Erin's cheek and handed her to Tara. He stood. "I guess I'll see you tomorrow."

Tara followed him to the door. Was she hoping he would stop and realize he needed to kiss her, too? Her hopes died quickly as he walked out and closed the door behind him.

It took every ounce of Tara's self-control not to run after him.

Matt braced an arm on his golf bag as Nick teed up his ball, then got set and proceeded to hit the ball, only to have his shot slice off to the left. Hearing the millionaire software genius's colorful words, Matt bit his lip to keep from smiling.

"Maybe a little instruction would help," Matt suggested.

"Damn, I told you I wasn't any good at this."

Matt put his tee in the ground. "You're not any good because you only play when you're feeling sorry for me or you have an argument with Cari." He looked at his friend. "You two aren't having a fight, are you?"

Nick shook his head.

"Good, because we'd never make it through the back nine. You'd be so anxious to get home and apologize."

"Hey, Cari and I are fine." Nick waved a hand. "I thought after what happened with Douglas, you might want to talk."

Matt gripped his club and took a practice swing, then lined up his shot. Using his body for power, he drove his ball off the tee.

Nick whistled. "It's nice to know that you're taking all this so well."

That wasn't the case. Matt had too much time on his hands. It made him realize how empty his life was without his career. "Hell, I hate it. But what can I do?"

"Well, I can tell you that the Malones are pulling

all their money out of Riverhaven until you are re-instated.''

Matt walked to his cart and slipped his wood into the bag. ''This is between Harry and me. He's never had any respect for me as a doctor. All I was to him depended on the money and publicity I bring to the hospital. He left me no choice.''

''So what are you going to do? And what am I going to do about Danny? If you go very far away—''

''Stop worrying, I'm not leaving medicine, or Danny. But I can't let Harry treat me this way. I'm tired of being jerked around.'' He grabbed the handle of his cart and started walking.

Nick went after him. ''And I don't blame you. Your life has been a mess this last year. You managed to continue working through it all. But I'd have to be blind not to see that Tara McNeal has put a gleam in your eye.''

Matt knew he couldn't fool his friend, just as Nick hadn't fooled him when he fell hopelessly in love with Cari.

''There can't be anything between Tara and me.''

''I didn't ask if there was anything going on. It's damn obvious what's going on. Hell, Saturday night you two were sizzling out on the dance floor.''

Matt continued walking, feeling the heat creep up his neck.

''Hell, I couldn't get Cari's attention, she was so interested in watching the two of you. I have to say I was more than a little jealous—that is, until I got her home.'' He cleared his throat. ''Have you convinced Tara to stay in Santa Cruz?''

Matt nodded. ''She's staying, but only to finish out

her commitment at the day-care center and to help me find my evil twin, then she'll be returning to Phoenix in August, as planned.''

Nick shook his head. ''I take it your decision has something to do with old wounds from the past.''

A long time ago, before Cari and after drinking too many beers, Matt and Nick had talked about their pasts. Nick's wife deserting him and Danny. Matt's biological mother abandoning him. They even discussed the worst time in Matt's life, when Julie broke off their engagement. Nick Malone knew more about him than anyone else.

Everything—except that he couldn't father a child. Matt had only said he wasn't cut out to have a family. ''I can't help how I feel.''

''It's a shame. Nice-looking woman, Tara McNeal. I had a feeling there was something starting up between you two. Take it from someone who knows, love is the best thing in the world. And your putting up a fight on this is futile. Just admit it, you want the woman.''

Matt definitely didn't want to admit anything about Tara, especially how empty his bed had been last night without her there. He didn't want to admit how lonely he would be when she left town for good. Mostly he didn't want to admit how she'd gotten under his skin and into his heart.

No, he wasn't going to admit anything. If he did he'd only be destroyed when Tara walked away. And she would. Experience had taught him that.

Tara had time to change her clothes and feed Erin a bottle before Matt came for them. He put the baby into the safety seat in his big sedan, and they headed downtown. Although the ride was quiet, Tara didn't feel uncomfortable with Matt, not until he touched her.

As he helped her out of the car, his hand seemed to burn through her skin. "Thank you," she managed to say. Then she hurried to busy herself with Erin. Today she'd decided on the canvas carrier, and strapped her niece against her chest. Then she put a bonnet on Erin to protect her from the sun. "We're ready." She grabbed the large shoulder bag with an extra bottle and diapers and started to put it on her shoulder. Matt took it from her.

"I can handle this." He tossed the strap over his broad shoulder. "Come on. We'll get this business out of the way. Then we can enjoy ourselves."

He guided her out of the parking lot to the street. They walked down a block past several specialty stores until they found the Jewel Box. Matt pushed open the door and allowed Tara to step inside ahead of him.

A balding, middle-aged man looked up from behind the glass cases. He smiled. "May I help you?"

Matt walked to the counter. "I hope so." He pulled the ring box out of his pocket. "I believe this was purchased here."

The man opened the velvet box, slipped on a pair of glasses and examined the emerald and diamond ring inside. "Why, yes. This was one of ours. I remember it because we'd just gotten it in on consignment that same day it was sold." He frowned. "Is there a problem?"

"No, no problem," Matt said. "I was just wondering if you remember who bought it?"

The man studied Matt, then glanced around the

empty shop. "I really can't give out our customers' names."

Matt wasn't happy the man didn't want to cooperate, but he understood. He pulled a copy of his credit card bill from his pocket, and a business card from Detective Warren. "I'm asking because my stolen credit card was used in the purchase. For the past year a man has been posing as me." Matt pulled out his driver's license. "You see, I'm Dr. Matthew Landers. The man who bought this ring was an imposter."

"Oh, I'm sorry, sir, but we're not responsible. Your credit card company can help you—"

"I didn't say you were responsible," Matt interrupted, taking a breath to stay calm. "I'm asking if you can describe the man."

Matt felt Tara's hand on his arm, and he glanced at her. She smiled at the salesman.

"I'm sorry, Mr...."

"Heger. Oliver Heger."

"Well, Oliver, I'm Tara. As you can understand, Dr. Landers is upset. This imposter has destroyed his credit and good standing in the community." She brightened her smile. "If there is anything you can do, we would greatly appreciate it."

The man glanced at Erin. "Cute baby."

Tara turned so the man could get a look at the baby. "Well, we think so." And as if on cue, Erin cooed.

Slowly Oliver's attention went to the question. "If I remember correctly, the man was young. In fact, I thought he was a little too young to be a doctor. Oh, yeah, I remember. He had an attitude. I was busy that day, and he was in this big hurry, saying he had to get back to the hospital. He was an intern.''

''Did he say what hospital?'' Tara asked as Matt jotted notes.

''Riverhaven.''

''What did he look like?''

''Well, he looked a lot more like a surfer than a doctor. Blond hair.'' He glanced at Matt. ''Not as light as yours. In fact I thought he had added some of those streaks to lighten it. His eyes were brown. His height was about five ten.''

''Anything else you can remember?''

''It was so long ago. I wish you'd come in sooner.''

''You did just fine, Oliver. If there is anything else you can remember, please call Dr. Landers, or Detective Warren at the police department. Anything would be a big help.''

''I will, I promise.''

Matt took the ring and slipped it in his pocket. He handed the man his business card. Then, before they had a chance to leave, Oliver called to them. ''If you and your wife are interested, I just got in the matching necklace and earrings to your ring.''

The salesman took a black velvet tray from a glass case. It held a perfect oval-cut emerald surrounded by tiny diamonds hung on an antique-gold chain. The matching earrings were a smaller version of the necklace.

Matt heard Tara's gasp. Oliver removed the necklace and held it up to her. ''The pieces are exquisite. The emerald is a perfect match for your eyes, Mrs. Landers.''

Tara seemed embarrassed. Was it Oliver's assumption of her being his wife? Matt's chest tightened at the thought.

"Well, thank you, Mr. Heger, for showing us the set. They truly are beautiful. We better go," Tara said.

She started for the door, but Matt was mesmerized by the necklace. Heger saw his interest.

"Come back again, Dr. Landers," he called as they walked out the door.

Tara looked at Matt. "I'm sorry that I didn't correct him about us being married, but he seemed more open to sharing information if he thought you were my husband."

Matt had no problem with the pretense. He only wished they'd gotten more information. "It was a good idea. You were the one who got him to talk, not me." Another dead end, he thought. "I should be thanking you."

"I think it was Erin who won him over."

"You're probably right." He bent and touched Erin's cheek. "You are a cutie, princess. Keep up the good work." He adjusted the diaper bag on his shoulder. "You want to look around town?"

Tara couldn't help but be excited at the prospect of spending the afternoon with Matt. "Sure."

When he placed his hand against her back, she wanted to lean into him but knew he was only being courteous. They were friends, Tara told herself. Nothing more.

For the next hour they walked along the boardwalk and watched Erin's fascination with the bright lights and the bells and loud sounds coming from a video-game area.

Soon Erin's interest faded, and she became hungry. They found a bench away from the noise and traffic, and Tara pulled a bottle from the bag and began to feed Erin. Matt tucked a blanket around the baby to make sure she was warm. Together they watched the sun sink slowly over the ocean.

"She's been good today," Matt said.

Tara smiled. "Erin's a good baby. Well, other than that early tooth that she got last week, she hasn't given me any trouble. And believe me, from day one, I've been flying blind." She laughed, remembering the first miserable days.

"Becoming a sudden mother had to be a shock," Matt said as he stretched out his long legs, his thigh muscles flexing under worn denim. Tara drew a breath, recalling the gentle strength of this man.

"You're telling me. I didn't have anything ready for a baby. If it wasn't for my neighbor Mrs. Lynch, I don't know what I would have done. She found me a crib and collected some baby clothes from her church. She even stayed with me during the first few days, so I would know how to make formula and get Erin on a schedule. You can't believe how many things there are to know about a baby."

Matt stared toward the ocean. "I know a little."

"Well, of course, you're a pediatrician."

"Being a parent is different," he replied.

Tara studied the handsome profile. His straight nose, his mouth. She thought again about the searing kisses they'd shared, the desire that had sparked between them. The man did know how to kiss. So why wasn't he married? Surely he'd been in love. "How come you've never married and had any kids of your own?"

She saw him tense, and for a minute thought he

wasn't going to answer. "I was engaged once. A long time ago." He looked at her, his dark eyes sad and distant. "But she decided she wasn't cut out for a life with me. We ended things before I finished my residency."

He'd loved a woman so much that he never had another relationship. Tara knew better than to grasp at the silly hope she could make Matt forget the woman. She'd had her night in his arms.

"What about your parents? Do they still live in the Midwest?"

"They did, but they're gone now."

"I'm sorry," Tara said and moved Erin to her shoulder and began patting her on the back.

"Mom and Dad were well into their forties when they adopted me. Dad was eighty-one when he had a stroke. He only survived a few days. Mom died in her sleep within the year. I think she didn't want to live without Dad."

Tara sighed, envying his loving parents. "I guess we've both lost our families."

"Are your parents gone?"

"My mother is, but I have no idea where my father is. He left us about fifteen years ago."

"Sorry. I didn't mean to dig up bad memories."

"You didn't," Tara said, but the old hurt surfaced anyway. "I accepted a long time ago that my dad didn't want us. He was busy running after his next big dream. For a long time he swept his family along with him, then one day he left and didn't come back." Tears threatened, and she angrily blinked them away.

"That's rough."

"I got over it. But I don't think my mother or Briana ever did."

Matt scooted closer to her, resting his arm along the back of the bench. "But they had you, Tara. You were there for them. But who's been there for you?"

Her eyes met his. Big mistake. His dark depths held hers. "I was old enough to take care of myself." She glanced away.

He touched her chin with his finger and turned her face to him. "We all need someone, sometime. Life is tough and it's hard to go it alone."

She shrugged. "Isn't that what you're doing?"

His eyes draw her with the loneliness she saw in their depths. "Some of us don't have much choice."

"We all have choices."

"Oh, Tara. How I wish that were true." He leaned down and placed a soft kiss against her lips.

Tara froze but allowed herself the luxury of the sweet kiss. All too soon he pulled back.

"We should get home," he whispered.

The ride home was quiet. Erin dozed in the back seat. Tara sat in the front, quickly coming to the conclusion that no matter how much distance she put between herself and Matt, she was still totally, hopelessly in love with the man.

## Chapter Eleven

Tara spent the next few days trying to stay out of Matt's way. Tara was at the center most mornings, but that didn't stop her thinking about him, wondering how he was coping.

At the end of the week, she arrived at the house to find Matt digging a flower bed in the backyard. Tara paused to admire the well-built man, minus his shirt and only wearing a pair of shorts. Each time Matt shoveled the soil, his muscular back and arms flexed, glistening from the sweat of his labor. Oh, my. He was beautiful.

Juanita's voice broke into her reverie. "He certainly is a pleasant man to look at."

Tara jerked her head around to see the older woman smiling.

"Yes, he is."

Matt spotted her, jabbed his shovel into the soil

and came to her. "Save me, Tara. Juanita is a slave driver."

"Come on, now. I'm just trying to keep you from getting lazy and fat. You can't sleep all morning, then lay around the house all day. If you're not working, then you need to stay active." She put her hands on her hips. "Have you forgotten you're a heart doctor?"

"Of course not," he said. "But just because I slept in one morning is nothing to panic over. I'm not out of shape. Right, Tara?"

Tara swallowed. "Right. You're fine." She couldn't look at his chest, but she remembered every inch of it. The swirl of light hair, the flat nipples that beaded so readily when she used her tongue.... Her body grew warm, and there was a sudden ache low in her stomach. She looked at his face, and something flickered in his darkened gaze. Had he suspected what she'd been fantasizing about? "They say working in the soil is good for your mental health."

Matt rolled his eyes. "There's nothing wrong with my health, mental or otherwise." He stalked toward the house.

Juanita sighed. "I was hoping I could distract him by keeping him busy. Darn that Harry Douglas anyway. Dr. Matt is the best doctor that hospital ever had. They have no right to treat him this way. And what about his patients? They need him most of all."

"What is Matt doing about his patients?" Tara asked.

"Another doctor is handling his caseload." Juanita glanced at the turned-over soil. "Now I'll never get my flowers in."

"Just let me change clothes and I'll help you."

"You don't have to. You've been working all morning."

"Cooped up inside," Tara said. "Erin and I need a little sun time, huh, cutie?"

The baby kicked.

"Oh, and I got something for Erin today." Juanita went into the house and appeared with a bright yellow baby swing. "A friend's granddaughter outgrew it and said Erin could use it."

Tara smiled and unstrapped the baby from the carrier. "This is wonderful. Thank you. Lookie, Erin, at what we have for you." With the swing anchored in the lawn, Tara lifted the baby into the seat. A canopy kept the sun from her face. Juanita cranked the handle and set the swing in motion.

Erin let out a squeal of delight, and both Juanita and Tara laughed.

"I wish all problems were this easy to solve," Juanita said. "I'm so worried about Dr. Matt. His career and that hospital have been his life. He needs to get back there, or at least find something else to occupy his time."

"Or something to occupy his time," Tara repeated. She thought for a moment, and suddenly it hit her. "Juanita, do you have any hot dogs in the house?"

"Hot dogs? No. Why?"

"Well, I think tonight would be perfect for a beach party. I've never been to one, and Matt said I should take advantage of my stay here. I think we should invite a few people. If that's not too much trouble for you."

"Please, give me trouble." Juanita hurried into the house and returned with a cordless phone, a notepad and a pencil. She punched out a phone number, then handed the phone to Tara. ''The Malones.''

After talking to Cari, Tara had most of the plans made. Nick and Cari were on their way over, bringing their swimsuits, a supply of hot dogs to grill for eight people.

Juanita was excited, too. ''Oh, Tara, you are a blessing. Too bad a certain doctor hasn't realized what's right under his nose.''

The older woman went into the house, leaving Tara to wish for the same. But it had been a long time since she wished for anything. She wondered if she remembered how.

The usually deserted beach Matt came to for quiet solitude was filled with laugher and children's voices. Seated in his low beach chair, he wondered how this had happened. He watched Tara and the three Malone children as they marched down the beach playing follow the leader.

The leggy, redheaded nymph had the kids jumping in the waves and dancing along the shore, including eight-year-old Danny, who always complained he was too old to play with his younger brother and sister. The boy had a big crush on Tara. Who didn't?

Suddenly little Matthew fell in the wet sand. Tara rushed to the crying toddler, and soon she had him laughing again. Matt's chest grew tight as he looked at the woman who would be the perfect mother. She needed children. Lots of children.

Nick dropped into the chair next to Matt's and handed him a soda. ''Glad to see someone else is doing a good job of keeping my brood in line.''

''I'd say she has them mesmerized.''

"Anything, as long as I can have a break."

"Why, Mr. Malone, I thought you loved every minute you spend with your kids."

"I do, but I wish I could have more time with their mother. It's not easy to find private time."

Matt had no sympathy for this man who seemed to have everything. A beautiful wife, money, children.

Matt glanced at the swing that held little Erin. When she began to fuss, he lifted her and carried her to his chair. "Do you feel left out, princess?" She stopped fussing and smiled at him.

"Oh, brother, are you in trouble," Nick groaned. "Not only does Tara have you running in circles, the baby does, too."

Matt wasn't going to deny it. But he knew that it was only temporary. A few more weeks and Tara was on her way back to Phoenix. He was determined to enjoy the time he had left.

Cari appeared at her husband's side. "I hope you aren't feeding Matt horror stories about marriage and kids."

"Who, me?" Nick put his arm around his wife and pulled her close. "Our marriage is great. I just wish I had more time with you."

"I save all my evenings for you," Cari said.

The couple's eyes met, and Matt could see the communication they shared without saying a word. Then Cari whispered something in her husband's ear. Matt was the one who blushed and looked away, only to see a soaked Tara coming up the beach with three wet and shivering kids. She had borrowed one of Cari's suits. The blue-green one-piece suit not only showed off her eyes but her long legs, too.

"I think we need to start a fire," she said.

Cari grabbed a towel and covered Krissy, then handed one to Danny.

Matt took care of Tara. Still holding Erin, he managed to wrap a towel around her while she was holding little Matthew. He looked at her, seeing her wet hair pulled back from her fresh-scrubbed face. He was overwhelmed by her natural beauty. "Cute freckles. But you better take the kids up to the house and put on warm clothes. I'll get the fire going for the hot dogs."

"I'm looking forward to it." She smiled and gathered the kids.

"I get to cook my own," Danny called as he ran toward the steps.

"So do I," Krissy added as she ran after her brother.

An argument started, but Tara smoothed things out before they'd made it to the top of the stairs.

Matt went to the fire ring and set a flame to it. But the heat didn't compare to what was going on inside his body.

Cari appeared with a tiny hooded sweatshirt for Erin. "Tara's quite a woman. And great with kids," Cari said as she dressed the baby.

Matt looked at her. "If you're trying to be subtle, it's not working."

"I just want you to be happy, and I think Tara's the woman who can make that happen."

*So do I,* he thought. "I'm not looking to settle down."

"Well, too bad for you. Because the look in your eyes says differently."

"Cari, I care about Tara, but that doesn't mean we

have to rush out and get married. I don't even have a job right now." Matt didn't want to know any of this. It only made things harder. "Love isn't always the answer to everything. Trust me, it wouldn't work between us."

"That's what I thought with Nick. Look at what we had to overcome." Cari touched Erin's cheek. "If you truly love each other, then you can handle anything that comes along."

Oh, how he wanted to believe that, but he was scared to chance it.

Tara returned with the kids all bundled up just in time to roast hot dogs. Juanita joined them, bringing potato salad and chips. They all sat eating as the sun sank over the ocean. Erin finished her bottle and went right to sleep.

The Malone children roasted marshmallows, and by the time they finished, they were all sticky. Nobody cared as they sat on the blanket and Nick and Matt told ghost stories. Little Matthew fell asleep and Matt covered him up, then he went to sit with Tara. She was surprised when he pulled her against him and wrapped his arms around her.

"You cold?" he asked.

"A little." She didn't want him to stop touching her. They talked quietly for a while and listened to the surf. All the time Matt was rubbing his hands up and down her arms.

Finally Nick and Cari gathered their kids and headed to the car. Everybody got hugs, then Matt stood with Tara as they waved goodbye.

He walked her to the cottage. "It was a great evening," he said. "Thanks for planning it."

"I'm glad you had a good time. We did force a party on you."

"You never have to worry about the Malones being forced on me. They're friends."

"They're like family," Tara added, knowing she felt the same way. Cari was her friend, too. "I'm going to miss them when I leave."

Matt walked her up the steps. He held Erin's carrier. "I guess we wore out the princess."

"She had a ball. All that attention from the kids."

They went inside. Matt took the baby to the crib and placed her inside. She didn't even stir. "Looks like she's down for the night."

Matt turned and found Tara watching him. He ached to go to her and take her in his arms. "Tara, I want to say something about what happened the other night."

She blinked, her heart racing. "What?"

"I just want you to know that even though I didn't use protection when we made love, I don't want you to worry about…anything. I haven't been with anyone in a long time." He shook his head. "And I've never before been foolish enough not to use a condom. I'm sorry."

She couldn't stop the heat rushing to her face. "It's okay, Matt."

"It's not okay." He came to her and gripped her arms. "It's not okay that I was irresponsible. It's not okay that you had me so crazy that I couldn't think about anything but being inside you."

"Matt—"

Before she could say a word his mouth covered hers in a heated kiss. A kiss that he'd been aching for since she'd come home from work. When she made a whimpering sound, he pulled her against him. He wanted her. But reality hit. He couldn't have her. Ever.

He released her and looked at her wide green eyes, then her swollen lips. "Sorry. Seems like whenever I'm around you I can't keep my hands to myself."

"It's okay, Matt."

"No, it's not. I promised you I wouldn't try to seduce you, and here I am all over you."

"It's just a kiss, Matt."

He raked his hand through his hair, trying to keep from touching her again. "It still shouldn't have happened." He took a deep breath. "Jim called and left a message while we were on the beach. Cathy and her husband are back from their vacation, and she's agreed to talk with us."

"That's great."

He raised an eyebrow. "So you'll go with me to San Diego?"

"Sure. When are you going?"

Matt looked relieved. "I thought we'd go the day after tomorrow, Saturday. Then you won't have to take any time off from the center. We can fly down and stay overnight and come back Sunday. If you'd like, we can sightsee. San Diego is a beautiful city with plenty to do. We'll only be gone about twenty-four hours. If you're uneasy with that, we can make the trip in one day like L.A. And about taking Erin, I've already talked with Juanita, and she offered to watch her for you."

Tara hesitated. "I want to go. Are you sure Juanita wants to watch her that long? It would make the trip easier if we don't have a baby."

He nodded. A lot of things would be easier. Matt

worried about how hard it was going to be to keep his promise to treat Tara like a friend only. Could he spend a weekend with Tara and not touch her? Right now that seemed damn impossible.

A little after noon on Saturday, Tara walked with Matt through the San Diego Airport with the hope that this trip would give them the answers they needed. For both their sakes.

A mid-size car was waiting for them at the curb. Matt tossed their bags into the back seat then drove to Coronado Island, to a converted mansion called the Glorietta Bay Inn.

He pulled into a parking space. "Do you have any objections to staying with me in a suite? Since it's a summer weekend and all, it was all they had left."

Tara couldn't stop the heat rushing to her face. Foolish as it was, she had no objections at all. "No, there's no problem."

"You sure? I don't want you to be uncomfortable."

"It's fine. I'm sure we can stay out of each other's way."

He nodded, then climbed out of the car. They registered, then Matt carried their bags through the ornate entry hall of the old Spreckel's Mansion to the back of the hotel. The walkways had covered lattices adorned with colorful blossoms. An outside entrance led to a staircase to their suite. Upstairs was a large living room, a small kitchen—and only one bedroom.

"The bedroom is yours," Matt said hurriedly, sensing her panic. "I'll sleep out here on the Hide-A-Bed." He tossed his suitcase on the sofa, then pulled a notebook from his jacket. "I'm going to call Cathy. Or do you want to?"

"No, you can." Tara walked to the bedroom and dropped her bag on the queen-size bed, then sank onto the mattress. Suddenly she felt shaky. What was she doing here? The man didn't want her. He as much as told her that. But she couldn't resist being close to Matt.

And once again she would be close to him—so close that she probably would hear his breathing when he fell asleep. Just like the night they'd made love....

*Stop it,* she ordered herself, and shot off the bed. They were here on business. That was the only reason. She had to stop fantasizing about what would never be. She worked the zipper on her suitcase and pulled out a pair of gray slacks and a pink shirt and hung them in the closet. Then she shook out a simple gauzy black dress and wondered what had possessed her to bring it.

*What do you think the man's going to do?* she asked herself. *Take you out and wine and dine you?*

There was a knock on the partially open door.

Tara looked up and saw Matt in the doorway.

"Cathy said we could stop by tomorrow afternoon."

Realizing she was holding the dress, she dropped it on the bed. "I thought she said we could see her today."

"I did, too, but her husband had made plans to go sailing that she didn't know about. Cathy apologized for the delay." Matt crossed his arms. "What do you think about taking a harbor cruise?"

"A cruise?"

"Well, we have the whole day to ourselves. Why waste it? If you'd rather, we could drive down to Tijuana. They have a lot of bargains."

She burst out laughing. "I don't think I need anything from Tijuana."

He snapped his fingers. "I know, how about the zoo?"

Excitement raced through her. "I've never been to a zoo. Can you believe it?"

"Then grab your walking shoes, my lady. We're heading to the best zoo in the country."

"Matt, you don't have to take me to the zoo. If you just want to relax…"

He stepped inside the bedroom, and his gaze burned into her. She could feel his heat as he gripped her shoulders and pulled her close. "There are a lot of things I want to do with you, Tara McNeal, and none of them are the least bit relaxing. So the zoo will be the safest place for us. I suggest we get out of this room. Now."

Tara's breathing grew labored. Oh, how she wanted to challenge him. Instead she grabbed her sweater and purse and headed toward the door.

The next three hours were spent walking around the zoo. Tara wanted to see it all, and Matt wanted to show her everything. He took her hand as if he'd done it a thousand times before, and together they wandered around the park. He refused to think about anything else. He only wanted to enjoy Tara's excitement as she went from one animal exhibit to another.

And he did. In fact, Matt hadn't realized what he'd been missing for so many years. He'd spent so much time working that he hadn't taken time to enjoy the simple things in life. The last thing he should let himself do was want Tara. But he did, so much. He had to keep telling himself that their time together would soon come to an end, and he would have to say goodbye to her. He promised himself he could handle that, too.

But today he was going to savor every minute.

It was nearly six when they arrived at the room. Even though they were both a little tired, Matt knew better than to stay cooped up in the suite with temptation. He suggested dinner across the street at the Del Coronado Hotel.

"Oh, Matt. That's so expensive. This trip is costing you so much. And since you're not working..."

"Hey, I'm on *paid* leave from the hospital," he explained, but he was tickled she was worried about him spending money.

"Oh."

He stared at her kissable mouth, which formed a perfect *O,* and his entire body went rigid.

"So," he said, trying to remember how to speak. "I think I can afford a weekend away. Now, I'm asking you out for dinner." He smiled. "I'm dying to see if that black dress looks as good on you as I think it will."

"It does," Tara said, unable to hide her blush.

"Good, then you better hurry up and put it on, I'm getting hungry."

"I'll just take a quick shower." She gathered her robe and toiletries and disappeared into the bath.

Twenty minutes later, after Matt had showered and dressed, Tara walked out of the bedroom. He turned around and his breath caught.

Tara's little black dress showed off her shoulders,

baring soft, flawless skin. The elastic top made the sleeves puff out and also accented her breasts. Matt remembered those beautiful breasts with the rosy colored nipples that beaded under his attention. He swallowed and forced his gaze to the full skirt that hit her mid-calf, drawing attention to her trim ankles. Her narrow feet were encased in strappy sandals, exposing her red-colored toenails.

Lord help him. He shook his head. "I was wrong, you look better than I ever imagined."

"Thank you," she said shyly. "Cari helped me pick it out. She said the material would be great for traveling."

Why did he get the feeling his friend knew exactly what she was doing when she'd found this dress? And traveling had nothing to do with it. "Remind me to thank Cari."

Tara's heart pounded as she looked at Matt, wearing tan slacks and a powder blue dress shirt. He walked past her, and she caught a whiff of his subtle aftershave. Her knees went weak. Oh, my, how was she going to make it through tonight?

"You look nice yourself," she said.

"Thank you. You ready?"

She nodded, then grabbed her shoulder bag.

They walked through the courtyard, Matt's hand against her back, then made their way across Orange Avenue, the main street on the island. They approached the Del Coronado Hotel, a huge white wooden structure with a famous red roof decorated with tiny fairy lights. They entered the elegant lobby with ornate architecture, but nothing prepared Tara for the Crown-Cornet Room. The massive dining room was as elegant as the name implied. The wooden beamed ceiling rose high and regal over the diners, the crystal chandeliers sparkling like stars in the sky.

"It's beautiful," Tara said.

"I'm glad you like it. I was here once on a medical conference. The food is excellent."

Matt took her hand and they followed the waiter across the room to a snowy-white linen-draped table by a window.

Tara couldn't help but wonder if Matt had brought a woman on the other trip. She shook away the thought.

They were seated, and the waiter handed them both menus before departing.

"What do you suggest?" Tara opened the large folder.

"The fish, of course. Unless you prefer pasta, or the dreaded red meat."

"Careful, Doctor, your credentials are showing."

"Sorry, I forgot I'm off duty."

Tara ignored the exorbitant prices and decided she wasn't going to worry about anything, not tonight. "Well, healthy eating can be delicious, too." She closed the menu and looked up as the waiter seemed to magically reappear. "I'll have the halibut," she told him.

"And I'm having the lobster," Matt said.

After the waiter left, Matt turned his attention to Tara. "I enjoyed this afternoon. It had been years since I visited a zoo."

"I enjoyed it, too," she said, remembering her dad had promised to take her many times.

"Well, I'm glad I could take you today."

"Thank you," she said, her voice suddenly husky

as his dark eyes locked with hers. This was getting dangerous. She glanced away and reached for her water glass to help ease her suddenly dry throat.

"How has your hand been healing?" Reaching across the table as she released the glass, he cupped her hand in his large palm. He put on his professional demeanor, but Tara still had trouble not reacting to his touch as he checked the fading scar that circled her thumb and part of her palm. "Does it bother you at all?" he asked.

*Only when you're touching me.* She shook her head. "The wound itched for the longest time." His warmth was sending shivers up her arm. "I barely notice it now." She tugged her hand away and rested it in her lap.

"You were lucky there wasn't any nerve damage. Your cut was pretty deep."

She pushed a strand of hair behind her ear. "Have I thanked you for coming to my rescue?"

He smiled. "Several times."

Tara looked at her dinner companion. Matt Landers was so much more than a handsome man and a dedicated surgeon. He was a nice person. "Not many people would give a stranger a place to stay—in his home. I think you might have had something to do with my getting a job." She cocked an eyebrow. "Was it all just to keep me in Santa Cruz?"

He took a drink of water. "Partly, and selfishly so. You've given me several leads. I would never have been able to talk with Bri's neighbor Lori without the address book." He shrugged. "And tomorrow, we're going to see Cathy Pennington."

"I just hope you're not disappointed."

"Think positively, Tara. This guy has to make a mistake sooner or later."

"I vote for sooner," she said as the waiter set their salads on the table.

Dinner was wonderful, and both felt too full when they finished. Matt suggested a walk. They ended up downstairs, going through the hotel's many shops, then went outside to the glass-enclosed terrace that overlooked the ocean. After sitting quietly together for awhile, Matt suggested they go down to the beach.

Not wanting their time to end, Tara agreed. The night was dark, with only the moonlight to guide them. They shed their shoes, and it seemed as natural as breathing for Matt to take her hand. They strolled farther and farther from the hotel lights. The breeze ruffled her hair and caused goose bumps to raise on her arms. Matt pulled her close, holding her against his body.

"Are you cold?"

"No, I'm fine."

"You look beautiful tonight."

She whispered, thank you, then silence stretched between them as they continued to walk the deserted beach. Words were unnecessary. Finally their steps slowed and Matt turned to her. She couldn't see his face, but she heard his rapid breathing as he lowered his head to hers.

His lips were soft but firm and tasted of desire. Quickly the kiss turned fervent as he coaxed her lips apart and his tongue moved inside. She dropped her sandals and wrapped her arms around his neck. She meshed her body to his, feeling his arousal against her stomach.

This time Matt groaned as his hands moved over her waist, then up her rib cage to her breasts. He squeezed the flesh as she leaned into his palms, causing her nipples to harden.

"Matt," she cried and gasped for air.

"I'm here, Tara." His fingers dipped into the top of her dress, caressing her bare skin, then he lowered his head and kissed her there. Again and again. "You, in this dress, have been driving me crazy all evening. I know I promised to keep my distance, but I can't. I want you."

She cradled his head against her body, loving the feelings he was creating. "Oh, Matt. I want you, too."

His mouth captured her again, searing her with a heat that burned clear down to her bare toes. He finally pulled away when they heard voices. He held her close and straightened her dress. "Let's go back to the room."

She nodded. He picked up their shoes and took her hand. The walk back was only ten minutes but seemed like an eternity as they made their way through the tourist-filled courtyard and across the street.

Finally at their hotel, Matt unlocked the door and ushered Tara inside. As soon as he turned the latch, he pulled her into his arms. His mouth came down on hers in a hungry attack. He drank from her mouth as if he were dying of thirst. "If you've changed your mind, you'd better stop me now," he warned. "I'm dying for you, Tara."

His words thrilled her. "I don't want you to stop," she said, busy working the buttons on his shirt.

Somehow they managed to make it up the steps

and into the bedroom. Matt's shirt dropped to the floor, and he tugged the top of her dress down to her waist.

With only a dim light from the bedside lamp, he stood back and looked at her. "You're perfect," he breathed, then reached out and cupped her breasts in his hands. He lowered his head and drew the nipple into his warm mouth, and the nub hardened instantly. She cried out.

"You like that, do you?" he said with satisfaction.

"Ooh, yes," she agreed, then realized she could give him something, too. Tracing her hands over his chest, she found the flat nipples nearly hidden beneath a swirl of golden hair. Then her tongue flicked over the sensitive skin until he was moaning her name.

Soon Matt had her dress around her ankles and was helping her to step out of it. All she had on were a pair of panties as he lay her down on the bed. Matt stood back, and the light caught his magnificent silhouette. Tara eagerly watched as he removed his trousers, then her gaze moved over his body, his flat stomach, narrow hips, his arousal. Finally her gaze met the desire in his eyes, and her arms reached out for him.

"I want to make you happy, Tara." He lay down beside her.

"All I need is you."

He took over then as his lips met hers in a searing kiss, leaving them both breathless. "I'm crazy for you. I can't think of anything else."

She smiled. "Perfect, because you're all I can think about."

He went on kissing her, working his way down

her cheek to her neck, her body. His hands stroked and teased until she thought she would die. "Please, Matt."

He raised up from the bed, grabbed his pants from the floor and removed a foil packet from his wallet. He rolled on the protection and returned to her.

He stripped off her panties, then moved over her as his mouth captured hers again. "I wanted to take this slow…to pleasure every part of you, but I want you too much."

"Love me, Matt," she begged.

His hand slipped between her legs, stroking her, finding her wet and ready. A purring sound came from deep in her throat as she lifted her hips in invitation.

Matt never had to fight so hard for control, and Tara wasn't making it any easier. Her sexy body wouldn't stop moving against his. How was a man supposed to think? But one look into those green eyes and he didn't want to think, he only wanted to feel.

"Matt…" she whispered.

He groaned as he pushed inside her wonderful warmth. Tara gasped and wrapped her long legs around him, pulling him deeper and deeper, and not just into her body. He felt like he was a part of her heart…her soul. And she was becoming a part of him. He shut his eyes and moved in the ageless rhythm that had him on the edge, praying he could give her heaven. As much as he tried to prolong the exquisite pleasure, he couldn't.

Soon he felt her tense, then watched her eyes grow large. His hand slipped between them. He stroked her until she came apart and he coaxed her through her climax. Then, before he could take another breath, he tumbled into paradise with her.

Matt felt Tara's arms hugging him tightly. He raised his head and looked at her. Her eyes filled with tears.

Trying not to panic, he asked, "Are you all right?"

She smiled. "I don't think I've ever been so all right—ever."

"That I will agree with," he said, then rolled over her and pulled her into his embrace. He was smiling, but his emotions were churning. It was too late. Tara had gotten into his heart.

Tara knew when Matt withdrew from her, not so much physically but emotionally. She raised her head. "Something tells me you're having second thoughts. If you're worried about me expecting anything…"

"No, it's not that, Tara. I just…there can't be any more…than this."

His words pierced her heart, but she couldn't let him see. She'd known from the first that Matt Landers could never give her what she wanted or needed. But dammit, why did it hurt so much?

She pulled herself together and sat up, drawing the sheet over her breasts. "Have I ever asked anything from you?"

He raked his fingers through his hair. "Dammit, Tara, you should. You should be demanding everything. Any man would be lucky to have you."

"Right now, I want to be with you." The sheet dropped as her hand moved to his chest and she traced her fingers over his skin.

"Tara, are you sure?"

"I'm sure. I want to be with you until…I have to leave." Her eyes met his bravely. "The question is, do you want to spend the time we have left with me?"

He cupped the back of her neck and pulled her down on top of him, searing her mouth with his hunger. By the time he released her, she was gasping for air.

"Never doubt that I want you. I've never wanted a woman more…ever."

Her heart sang with his confession. Now she just had to convince herself that all she wanted was his body—and keep her heart out of it.

"Show me," she whispered.

## Chapter Twelve

The next morning, Tara was awakened by Matt's kisses and soon he was coaxing her body into responding to his slow, sweet lovemaking. An hour later, he took her into the shower, where he taught her the advantages of water conservation.

Tara decided she'd never be able to get in a shower without thinking about what Matt had done to her with a bar of soap and his talented hands.

Somehow they managed to dress and pack. After checking out, they enjoyed the hotel's continental breakfast on the massive porch. But reality intruded. Tara called home and talked to Juanita. The older woman assured her Erin was doing fine and not to worry. Tara thanked her again for watching her and promised they would be home by nine that evening. After hanging up, she returned to the table and Matt.

He smiled as she sat down in the wrought-iron chair. "Is everything okay with Erin?"

She nodded. "I just miss her."

"Of course you do, you're her mother."

His statement made her smile. "I guess I am."

He took a sip of coffee. "You seem surprised. You're a great mother, better than a lot I've known."

"Have you known a lot of bad mothers?" Tara couldn't read his eyes. "Or are you speaking from experience? I mean you said you were adopted by wonderful people, but I remember you telling me your birth mother had abandoned you."

Matt leaned toward her. "I was only a few days old, Tara. How could I feel anything one way or the other?"

"We all have feelings, Matt. It doesn't matter how old you were. I mean, I know now how much my father's desertion affected Bri and…me." This was the first time she'd admitted that to anyone. "It's devastating for a child to think he or she isn't lovable enough to keep parents around." Too late she realized she was giving away too much about herself. "That's why it's so important that Erin knows she's loved, not just by me but her mother, too."

"And I received all the love I needed from my real parents, the Landerses. If possible, they nearly smothered me with too much love and attention. So don't feel sorry for me, Tara," he said, his voice growing cool. He sounded as if he were trying to convince himself. "Believe me, the last thing I want from you is pity."

Matt saw the pained expression on Tara's face and wanted to apologize, but it was better this way. Their magical weekend had to come to an end. It was back to reality.

He checked his watch. "You ready to go? I told Cathy we'd be there by eleven."

"Sure." Tara grabbed her purse, and they walked to the car.

Matt drove across the bridge to the freeway, then got off at an exit not far from the naval base. The Penningtons' brown-and-cream-colored town house was on a quiet residential street.

Matt parked along the curb then helped Tara from the car. Just touching her set off sparks, but he was more concerned about her nervousness. He gave her an encouraging smile. "It's going to be all right."

"What if this trip turns up nothing? What if it's a waste?"

His gaze locked with hers, and he knew that, no matter what, he would never forget this weekend, or loving Tara. "It's not a waste. At least you'll get to see an old friend." He checked the number on the building as they went up the porch. He knocked, and an attractive blonde opened the door and looked them over, then smiled in recognition. "Tara, is it really you?" Tears formed in the small woman's eyes, and she went into Tara's arms.

They separated, and Tara glanced over her, too. "Cathy, you look wonderful."

"I'm happy. Bob, my husband, is great."

"Good." Tara motioned to Matt. "This is Dr. Matthew Landers, Cathy. Matt, Cathy."

"I can't believe there are two of you." They exchanged a handshake. "Please, come inside," Cathy offered.

So she had known the imposter. Eagerly Matt followed Tara as they walked into a comfortable living room. There were several photos of the Penningtons on the bookcase.

"Sit down. Bob isn't here, he pulled duty today, but I wanted to talk to you without him around, anyway. He wasn't crazy about me going to Mexico with Bri when he was overseas. See, we were having a rough time when he got orders to ship out. I'm sorry, I haven't even offered you anything to drink."

"We're fine," Tara said as they took a seat on the sofa. "We can't stay long. But we wanted to visit and ask you some questions about Mexico."

"I'll tell you anything you want. I just didn't want to talk with that investigator or have Bob find out. He's pretty jealous. You know those Marines." Cathy tried to smile, but the sadness was evident in her eyes. "But Bri was important to me. I didn't know she was in trouble. I'm so sorry about what happened."

"I know you are, Cathy. You were her best friend."

The woman nodded. "The investigator said she had a baby, a little girl."

"Erin." Tara dug through her purse and pulled out a photo.

"Oh, she's cute. She looks like Bri. I knew she was pregnant, but the last I talked to her, she was going to find the father."

"We were hoping you could tell us more about this man who says he's Matt Landers. You did meet him on the trip?"

"Yes, briefly," Cathy said. "He didn't hang around me much. After meeting Bri, he only spent time with her."

"And he was introduced to you as Dr. Matthew Landers?"

"That's what Bri called him, but he sure didn't look like a doctor to me." She shrugged. "But, hey, the man was on vacation." Cathy rolled her eyes. "He was all she talked about. And they were together all the time. I guess I was jealous because that left me alone, but it all worked out, because their being together made me realize how much I missed Bob." She seemed to be daydreaming. "Can you imagine Bri with a stuffy doctor?" As if Cathy realized what she'd just said, a blush covered her cheeks. "Oh, I'm sorry, I didn't mean…"

Matt smiled. "No offense taken. I never had the pleasure of meeting Bri, but if she was anything like Tara, I'm sure I'd have liked her very much." Enough small talk, Matt thought. More information. "Do you remember what this man looked like?"

"You mean the man who was pretending to be you?" She frowned. "How weird is that?"

"It's made a mess of my life, so if you can tell me what this man looked like, I'd appreciate your help."

"Oh, I have a picture." Cathy jumped up as Matt and Tara exchanged a smile.

"It's the only one that Bob didn't destroy. Here, the guy's kind of cute, but I think you are much better looking."

Matt's hand was trembling as he focused on the amateur photograph. Recognition was instantaneous.

"Damn. I know him."

"Garrison Kellen. That's who stole my identity. Damn! Damn!" Matt hit the dashboard as Tara drove the rental car to the airport.

The second they had left Cathy's house, Tara took Matt's keys, knowing he was upset over the discovery. "Who is Garrison Kellen?"

"Would you believe until eighteen months ago he was an intern at the hospital?"

"You're kidding!"

"I wish." Matt drew a breath. "Gary wanted one of the two spots available for a surgical residency. I served on the review board making the decision. Gary wanted to be a surgeon, but during the time I worked with the man, I realized how inept he was. He might have made a fair doctor, but he didn't have the skill or dedication for surgery. I talked with him several times about changing the direction of his medical career. He told me surgery was all he wanted, and his father's money would make sure that he got it."

Tara gasped. "What happened?"

"Nothing. The other surgeons agreed with me, and the residency spots were awarded to more qualified doctors. Later, I heard that Kellen's father tried without success to buy his way in." Matt shook his head. "I have to give Harry credit for not caving in."

Tara found the exit to the airport and turned. "What I can't understand is if the Kellens had money, why did he steal your wallet?"

"He didn't want my money. He wanted to destroy me, Tara. It was my vote that decided his fate."

"You had to do what was right, Matt. It was your job." She touched his hand on the seat between them. "Now all you have to do is give Gary's picture to Detective Warren, and they'll handle finding him. It's all over."

"No, it's not." He glanced across the car at her. "Have you forgotten Gary Kellen is Erin's father?"

Tara spent the evening with Erin, letting her know how much she'd missed her. She didn't want to think about what happened today or how close they were to finding Erin's father. A man she truly never expected to find.

"Oh, Bri, is this what you wanted?" Tara whispered "Is it so important for Erin to know someone who doesn't care who he hurts, especially you?" She looked at the baby sleeping in the crib, wondering if the Kellens would try and take her away. Panic tore through her. They had money. They could fight for custody. And maybe win. Tears flooded her eyes. No, she wouldn't give Erin up. She couldn't.

There was a knock on the door, and Tara jumped. She opened the door and saw Matt standing outside.

"Oh, Matt. I'm so scared." She went into his arms. "I don't want to lose Erin."

He drew her close, and she rested her head against his chest. "You're not going to lose Erin," he said. "I won't let that happen, no matter what I have to do." He stepped back and made her look at him. "I've already talked to my lawyer, Ed Podesta. The courts are more lenient, awarding more rights to fathers. But if Kellen is convicted we won't have to worry, at least for awhile."

Tara's heart raced as she wondered about her niece's fate, afraid she wouldn't have any say about what was going to happen.

"Look, Tara, my name is on the birth certificate.

I could claim Erin as my child. Kellen never has to know he's her father.''

She loved him all the more. ''You would do that?''

He nodded. ''I would do anything to protect Erin.''

She hugged him. ''Oh, Matt. I wish I could, but I promised my sister. Besides, what about later? He might find out.''

''Come on, Tara. Bri had no idea that her baby's father was a thief.''

''But remember what you said about it being important to know who your parents are? Like you, someday Erin may ask about her mother and father.''

Matt knew she was right, but he was losing them both. Somehow he'd let Tara and Erin work their way into his heart. Now they were walking out of his life.

''Why don't we wait until Kellen is caught? Then I'll help you with whatever you need to do.''

''Thank you. We're lucky to have you.''

''You've helped me, too. It was the address book that led us to Cathy.''

''I'm glad we could help get your life back to normal. It shouldn't take long to find him, and then you can return to the hospital.''

None of that seemed important to Matt. Not when he wanted to pull Tara into his arms and beg her to stay with him. ''You have to know I'm not going to let anyone hurt you or Erin.'' *I love you,* he cried inside.

She nodded.

He watched the silent tears pour from her eyes. All he could do was hold her. He couldn't make any more promises. Soon this would be over and Tara would be out of his life, but she'd never be out of his heart.

"Miss Tara, look, I colored a picture of my mommy and daddy."

Tara forced a smile for four-year-old Ashley. "I can see that. It's very good," Tara encouraged as she leaned over the worktable at the center.

Five days had passed since Matt and Tara returned from San Diego. They'd shared meals and talked, but not about anything other than the investigation. Tara missed him coming to the cottage. Erin missed him, too.

"Miss Tara, Miss Tara. It's time for lunch," Timmy, another four-year-old, said. Tara glanced at the clock and discovered Matt standing outside her classroom. Her mouth went dry and her skin tingled at the mere sight of him. What was he doing at the hospital?

"That's right, children, it's time for lunch. Line up, and Rachel will take you in." Tara opened the door and called for a co-worker to come. Once the classroom was vacant, Matt came in.

"Hi."

"Hi, yourself. What are you doing at the hospital?"

"Seems I've been reinstated."

"Oh, Matt, that's wonderful." She reached for him, then realized what she was doing and backed off. "What happened?"

He smiled, and her heart did a somersault.

"Mrs. Chandler, one of the hospital board members, called me this morning and asked if I'd come in today and meet with her. It turns out that they now feel they made a rash decision in insisting I take a leave of absence. She apologized on behalf of the entire board and asked if I would consider coming back.''

"Of course you told them yes.''

"Yes, I did, especially after I learned that Harry Douglas will no longer be administrator. Mrs. Chandler also guaranteed that a lot of things are going to change at Riverhaven, including more security.''

"That's wonderful.'' She was happy for him.

"Juanita will be happy. When I left this morning she told me not to come home unless I had a job.''

They were both laughing when Tara looked up and saw Detective Warren walking toward them.

"Hello, Tara, Matt.''

"Hi, Tom.'' They shook hands. "Has something happened?''

"That's what I came to talk to you about. We finally caught a break and found Kellen.''

"How?'' Matt asked. "Where?''

The middle-aged man raised his hand. "We got lucky. He'd gone to his parents' home in San Francisco. He was bold enough to think he'd never be caught.'' A big grin split the detective's face. "But we got him.'' He turned to Tara. "Thanks to you, Tara. I can't tell you how much that address book helped us.''

"I'm just glad it's all over.'' But it wasn't. She still had one more challenge to face.

"Where are they holding him?'' Matt asked.

"He's in San Francisco, but they'll be bringing him down tomorrow to face fraud charges.''

"I want to be there," Matt said. "I have to see him."

"I don't blame you," Tom said, "but I have to warn you. His parents are rich, and they've hired some high-powered attorneys. One thing in our favor is the new laws on the books covering the use of someone's private information to obtain credit. I'm hoping, Matt, with your prominence in this community the DA will want to go for broke. After all, Kellen deliberately set out to destroy your reputation and career."

"I just want my name cleared and any debts he incurred while on his credit spree paid in full." He glanced at Tara. "A big court case will only hurt innocent people. Remember there's a child involved."

Tara couldn't stop shaking when they arrived at the police station. Matt stayed close by her side as the detective took them into his cubicle and showed three credit cards in Matt's name that they'd found in Gary Kellen's apartment during a search.

"We talked with his parents. Mr. Kellen was angry. Angry that his son had failed him once again. But the Kellens are used to getting what they want.

"His mother was devastated, of course, but tried to make excuses for him. She explained that her son has been spoiled all his life, but they never dreamed he had it in him to be so vindictive. Mrs. Kellen said to tell you she's sorry for all the trouble Gary's caused you."

"Do they know about the child?" Tara asked.

Tom shook his head. "That's up to you, Tara. If you ask me, your baby would be better off not knowing this man. There are hundreds of men who would gladly fill the dad role for that cute kid of yours. This Kellen is a selfish bastard.''

"I need to see him," she said. "If he finds out about Erin later, he could come after her." She glanced at Matt, pleading for help. "I have to tell him now."

Matt didn't want her to tell Kellen, either, but he knew she was right. "Just don't let him bully you into anything," he warned. "You have custody of Erin. He's the one who ran out on your sister."

She nodded, trying to work up courage. Then she felt Matt's hand on her shoulder. He was there for her. But for how long? The nightmare was almost over. Once things were settled, she should leave. That caused her more panic than the thought of seeing Kellen.

Tom stood. "Okay, then let's go and get this over with."

The detective took Tara and Matt into a room where a guard was posted and another man sat at a long table. He had brownish-blond hair cut in a shaggy style. His build was much smaller than Matt's. In fact, he was downright thin. His face was angular, and there wasn't a cleft in his chin. The two men didn't look anything alike. Tara looked hard and was grateful she couldn't see any resemblance to Erin, or maybe that was just wishful thinking on her part.

Kellen gave her the once-over, making her skin crawl.

"Kellen, there are two people here to see you."

Gary Kellen slouched in his chair. "I want my lawyer in here."

Tom nodded and went out. Moments later he returned with a man in his thirties, dressed in a custom-tailored suit, who stood next to his client.

Kellen grinned. "Well, Dr. Landers, I wish I could say it was good to see you."

"Wish I could say the same," Matt retorted. "Why, Gary? You had a good career going. Why did you blow it off?"

"What career?" he said. "You more or less said I was nothing but GP material. Hell, couldn't your ego risk someone competing with you?"

That struck Matt hard. "I'd never stand in the way of talent. But you didn't have that talent, the dedication it takes to be a surgeon. You didn't have the drive. Hell, most nights you couldn't even finish your shift at the hospital. Time and time again, you got other interns to cover for you. That's not what we want from surgeons at Riverhaven."

Kellen looked away. Matt was happy at least to see he appeared ashamed. "I don't need to be a doctor anyway," he said. "I just did it for my old man. It was his dream." He glanced at Tara again, then finally said, "Do I know you?"

Tara approached him. "No, you don't know me, but you knew my sister. Bri. Briana McNeal."

Something flashed in his eyes. "Hell, don't tell me she's after me, too."

"No, my sister isn't coming after you." Tara fought tears. "She died about four months ago."

"Then what do you want from me?"

"My sister died from complications during childbirth. She wanted me to find you and let you know that you have a daughter."

Kellen looked shocked at first, then he shot a

glance at Matt. "I bet it was quite a surprise when she arrived at your door and tried to hand you a kid. Oh, I wish I'd been there to see it. The great Dr. Landers trying to talk his way out of being a daddy."

In a split second, Matt was across the table and had Kellen by the shirt. "I'd like to work you over myself, but you're not worth the time. Besides, I doubt anything, even a beating, would get through to you." He released him. "The child is yours," he said.

"I don't want a brat." He looked at his lawyer. "Dammit, man, help me here. I can't give Dad something else to hang over my head." Kellen turned to Matt. "Hey, I bet your name is on the birth certificate. Am I right?" He grinned nastily.

"Are you saying you don't want any connection to your child?" Matt asked.

"Exactly. And don't try to get any money from me or my family."

"Then have your lawyer draw up a document saying you're giving up your parental rights."

Kellen signaled the lawyer. "Do it." He looked at Tara. "I'm sorry about Bri. We had a good time together."

Tara turned away. Matt could see her shaking.

"Okay, Kellen," Detective Warren said, "let's get you back in your cell."

The police officer escorted him out the door. Matt stopped the lawyer as he started to follow his client. "I want that document drawn up as soon as possible."

"I'll have it by tomorrow morning."

Matt handed him his business card. "Have it couriered to my home by noon. If I don't hear from you,

I'll have my lawyer on your doorstep. And we may be talking private lawsuit. Because thanks to your client, I have nothing to lose.''

The man nodded, then walked out.

Matt turned to Tara. That wasn't true, he had a lot to lose. He was about to lose the woman he loved.

Matt spent the rest of the day with Tara, but neither of them said much. Juanita took care of Erin, sad because the little girl would soon be leaving.

After a quiet dinner, Tara excused herself and took Erin to the cottage. Matt wanted to stop her but knew that she had to work through this.

"This is such a shame," Juanita said. "All this happening to such a sweet girl."

"Erin's just a baby. She'll be all right."

"I'm not talking about Erin, I'm talking about Tara. Her whole life has been turned upside down, and now she has to find a way to pick up the pieces and move on...alone."

"She'll be fine once she's back home in Phoenix."

"How can she be all right when her heart is breaking?" Juanita shook her head. "You men are so dense."

Matt had no idea what Juanita was talking about, but he was going to find out. He went to the cottage, but Tara and Erin weren't there. He stood on the edge of the rise and looked at the beach. There was only one person around, a tall, slender woman with her baby strapped against her as she walked barefoot along the shore.

He watched for a while, admiring the playful way she danced along the surf. Then she swung in a circle, and Matt could imagine that Erin was smiling at her mother's antics.

Tara, Erin's mother. Well, that was what she was now.

He walked down the steps, kicked off his shoes, then walked to mother and daughter. Tara stopped when she saw she wasn't alone.

"Matt, I didn't know you were there."

He smiled. "I just got here. I hope you don't mind. I wouldn't want to intrude."

"It's your beach. I just wanted to come here because I'm not going to have many more chances." She looked at the surf. "Erin and I will be leaving at the end of the week. I've already called Charlene at the center and told her."

His heart jumped to his throat, and he worked to swallow. "I don't see why you can't stay as planned. It's only a few more weeks."

Her eyes met his. "You know why, Matt. It's only prolonging the inevitable. It's better this way. It's better we don't hold out for expectations that neither one of us can meet."

"What expectations? I only asked you to stay a few more weeks."

"Why? So we can share a bed but nothing else?"

He felt like she'd hit him in the stomach. "I told you from the beginning I couldn't offer you what you needed."

She shook her head. "And I'm not asking for anything. I'm just stating facts. I can't play this game anymore, Matt. I was wrong to think I could." She drew a shaky breath, and Matt fought to keep from pulling her into his arms and begging her to stay. But once she discovered his secret, she'd leave anyway.

"Thank you, Matt." She forced a smiled. "Seems I've got a lot to thank you for. It's funny, but I'm not usually a needy person."

"We all need help sometime."

"Well, thank you again for yours, for opening your home to me and Erin and sharing your beautiful beach with me. You are a wonderful man." She stood on tiptoes and pressed her mouth to his. The kiss was so sweet, Matt wanted it to go on forever...and ever. But all too soon she pulled away.

"Goodbye, Matt." She turned and headed to the steps.

"Goodbye, Tara."

Matt's chest constricted, and he felt like he couldn't take the next breath as he watched her walk away. What kind of heart doctor was he, when he couldn't even do anything to stop the pain in his own?

## Chapter Thirteen

Cari Malone stood in Matt's office doorway. "I think you should seriously consider having your head examined."

He didn't bother to ask her why. He was pretty sure he already knew the answer. "Hello to you, too, Cari."

"Hello." Her expression softened as she walked in and closed the door. "I hope you aren't busy, because I need to hammer some sense into you. But, what the heck, anything to help a friend." She studied him for a moment. "One thing I can't figure out is how to go about it. Should I beat around the bush or just come right out and tell you how foolish you are to let Tara leave town?"

Matt raised a hand. "Why don't you save your breath and pretend you've already said it." He didn't need Cari to sell him on Tara. He already knew that she was the best thing that had ever happened to him…and he loved her like he never thought it possible to love a woman. "Some things are just out of our reach, Cari. Let's leave it at that."

Blowing out a breath, she leaned against the edge of the desk. "Funny, I don't remember you telling me that when I thought Nick and I were hopeless. No, you just worked tirelessly on getting us to see the light." She smiled. "Now I'm here to help you."

"That was different." If there were ever two people who belonged together, it was Nick and Cari. He got up and went to the window.

"Of course it was different," she agreed. "But that doesn't change the fact that you're hopelessly in love with Tara McNeal, and for some crazy reason you're letting her and that beautiful little girl walk out of your life."

His chest tightened and he had trouble taking a breath. "I have to, for their sakes. I'm not the man they need. My career comes first."

"I'm not buying it, Landers. So you better come up with something else. Because you have less than twenty-four hours before a woman who loves you…is gone."

He swung around. "You think I want that? You think I don't want her in my arms, in my life? But there are things…"

"Then tell her," Cari insisted. "That's what love is all about, Matt. Trust. Trust Tara's love to accept you, flaws and all." Cari gave him a knowing grin. "And if I'm any judge of character she's going to love you no matter what."

How he wished that were true. "There are things that I can't give her."

"Give her a chance to decide. Believe me, if you don't, you'll regret it for the rest of your life."

Tara was putting the last of her clothes into the suitcase. There wasn't much to pack, except for the things that Cari and Juanita insisted she take for Erin. No handouts, Tara told herself, but she knew that her friends had given these things out of love, not because they felt sorry for her.

Juanita walked into the cottage carrying Mexican sweet bread. "I thought you could use this for the trip. Just don't drive too long tonight." She hugged her. "Oh, Tara, I'm going to miss you and the *niña*."

Tara fought tears, but it didn't work. Juanita had come to mean so much to her. "I'm going to miss you, too. But I have to leave." She pulled away.

"But why? So many people here love you and little Erin."

Tara glanced away. *Matt doesn't love us enough to ask us to stay.* "I'm glad, but it's best for us to return to Phoenix."

"Before you say goodbye to Dr. Matt?"

Tara zipped her bag. "We've already said our goodbyes."

"Oh, you are as stubborn as he is. You care about each other, but for some crazy reason you can't say the words."

Hope shot through Tara. "What do you mean?"

"Are you blind, child? Dr. Matt loves you."

"Did he tell you that?"

The housekeeper shook her head. "He's worse than you. If you had any sense you'd go down to the beach and talk to him. Please, I know he wants you there."

Dare she hope? Was there a chance for them?

"Are you going to let Dr. Matt's stubbornness send you away?"

Juanita was right. She couldn't leave like this. Matt was going to have to send her away. "No."

A smile lit the older woman's face. "Good. You go. I'll watch Erin." She pushed Tara toward the door.

Within seconds, Tara was hurrying across the lawn to the wooden steps. After stripping off her shoes, she climbed down to the beach. Matt was easy to find as he walked along the shore about fifty yards away. "Matt," she called.

He turned toward her, and her breath caught as the summer breeze ruffled his light blond hair. His face was tanned with a healthy glow he'd gotten during his time off from the hospital. He had on khaki shorts and a long-sleeved T-shirt.

"Tara. Is something wrong?"

She swallowed, wishing for more encouragement from him. But she had to be brave. "No, I'm packed up and about ready to leave. I just…just wanted to say…" She couldn't seem to take her eyes off him. It was as if she were trying to memorize everything about the man she'd come to love. As if she would ever forget him. She came closer. "Thank you again for everything, for letting Erin and me use the cottage. For being there when we needed you."

He shrugged. "You're welcome."

"Well, I guess that's all." She wanted to cry. "Goodbye, Matt." She turned and started to the steps, praying he would stop her.

Matt's heart was pounding so loud it made his ears ring as he watched Tara go toward the steps…and out of his life. What life? He'd only existed before she arrived that day in his office. Suddenly he knew he couldn't let her go. "Tara, wait," he called.

She stopped and swung around, her beautiful face filled with hope. "What did you say?"

He swallowed. "I said wait."

"Why, Matt? Why don't you want me to go?"

He managed to get to her, all the time trying to remember what Cari had said to him about trust. "Because I can't go on without you." His voice turned husky. "Because I don't want to face the future without you."

She ran into his arms. "Oh, Matt,"

He watched her green eyes darken with desire. He tried to ignore the temptation, but he couldn't. He lowered his head and took her mouth. It was like he'd gone to heaven. She parted her lips, and he deepened the kiss as he pushed inside, hungry for what only she could give him, what he'd been starving for for days. Now he had everything. Or did he? He pulled back. "Tara, I need to tell you something."

"Later," she murmured as she offered him her inviting lips.

"No, now," he insisted, knowing he had to tell her his secret. He stepped back and drew a breath. "Tara, I want to give you everything."

"I don't want anything but you," she said.

He smiled. "Oh, lady, you have me. You had me the second you walked into my office. I love you more than I thought possible." He paused. "But it may not be enough." *Trust.* He kept hearing Cari's words. *Trust her.*

He saw her confusion but continued anyway. "I

know how much you want a family, Tara.'' His eyes burned. ''But I can't give you children.'' He swallowed hard. ''I'm sterile.''

He watched shock register on her face, and soon tears welled in her eyes. He couldn't deal with it.

''I guess that says it all,'' he said, then took a deep breath to keep his emotions in check. ''Well, I suppose you should get started on your trip home. Goodbye, Tara.'' He took off down the beach. He'd be damned if he was going to hang around to watch her leave him or see the pity in her eyes.

Tara stood frozen in the sand as Matt's words echoed in her ears. *I can't give you children.* No wonder he hadn't been worried about her getting pregnant. Because he couldn't. Disappointment surged through her, knowing she would never have a baby with the man she loved. And Matt. Oh, God, Matt. All this time he'd had this terrible secret locked up inside him.

She ran after him. Somehow she had to convince him that all she needed was him and his love.

''Matt, wait,'' she called.

He slowed, but didn't face her. She grabbed him by the arm, making him sit down in the sand.

''Matt, listen to me.''

He shook his head. ''It's okay, Tara. Really. I understand how you feel....''

''No, Matt, I don't think you do,'' she began. ''Because you never gave me the chance to tell you. You just took it for granted that I would walk out of your life. Worse, you let me think you didn't want me.'' She glared at him, ignoring his brooding brown-eyed stare. ''How dare you blurt out that you love me, then not trust me enough to share your pain.''

He drew a breath. ''Most women want children.''

''Most women want love, Dr. Landers.'' Tears flooded her eyes. ''I was so close to leaving town, and you'd never see me again. What about Erin, Matt? She needs you. You think that little girl cares that you aren't her biological father? You've been the only father she's ever known.'' She bit her trembling lips. ''She loves you, too.''

He looked toward the water, and she could read the agony in his eyes. ''I love her so much,'' he said as he tossed a piece of shell toward the water. ''God, Tara. I've watched you with the children at the center. You can't say you don't want your own.''

She remained silent. She ached to have her own child—his child. ''It's something we can deal with together, Matt.''

''Oh, Tara, I don't want you to regret giving that up.''

She had to get through to him. ''Matt, if you knew that I couldn't have any children, would that change how you feel about me?''

He never hesitated. ''No.''

''And you *don't* even know if I can have children. Yet you love me anyway.''

They sat for a moment, then finally Matt spoke. ''I blew it, didn't I?''

Her gaze met his beautiful brown eyes. ''The only way you could have blown it is if you'd let me leave. And you didn't.''

He smiled. ''I would have come to Phoenix to bring you back.''

She wrapped her arms around his neck. "Oh, I love you, Matt Landers."

"I love you, too, Tara McNeal." His mouth closed over hers in a hungry kiss that told her how much he loved and needed her. Releasing her mouth, he continued teasing nibbles down her cheek, to her neck.

"Do you think you could be happy living in Santa Cruz permanently with a doctor who works long hours?" he asked.

Tara pulled back. "Just what are you asking, Dr. Landers?" She needed the words.

"Will you marry me, Tara?"

Those were the words. "Oh, yes, Matt. I'll marry you."

He kissed her again and again as desire raced through them. Tara broke away. "Oh, my, we're getting a little carried away on a public beach."

"Just wait until later. I'm going to show you exactly how much I love you," Matt promised.

Tara shivered. "I'm going to hold you to that, Dr. Landers. But right now, we better get back to the house. I left Erin with Juanita."

Reluctantly, Matt released her and helped her up from the sand. He wrapped his arm around her waist and drew her to his side. "I guess we better let Juanita know that there's going to be a wedding—and soon."

"Soon," Tara agreed.

He leaned down and kissed the tip of her nose. "First, I guess we should ask Erin how she feels about her mommy getting married."

Tara had never heard any sweeter words. "Oh, I think she'll approve of her mommy marrying her new daddy."

## *Epilogue*

Six weeks later…

At sunset, Tara and Matt's marriage was to take place on the bluff above the beach. The Malones and Tara's co-workers from the center were all invited to the intimate gathering.

Tara stood in her tea-length ivory wedding dress. The sheer layers of material draped loosely over her tall frame, exposing just enough of her curves to keep a man interested. And Matt's intense gaze told her he was.

The ceremony began with soft music and little Krissy as the flower girl, then Cari went down the aisle and took her place as matron of honor while Nick stood as Matt's best man.

The music swelled as Tara started toward her new life, her new family. The man she loved. As long as Tara lived she would never forget the love in her husband-to-be's eyes as she walked toward the floral-covered archway.

The second Matt took her hand, she knew that whatever life dealt them in years to come, they would always have the most important thing, love. And she realized with love anything could happen, even miracles.

When the ceremony ended Matt kissed her passionately, promising her what was to come later. He finally released her to cheers from applauding guests who wanted to wish them well.

The reception immediately followed at the house, but Matt whispered to his new wife to be ready to leave within an hour, because that was as long as he could wait to have her to himself. Tara couldn't wait, either. She had a surprise for Matt, too. Tonight was going to be very special.

With Cari's help, Tara changed into her travel clothes, burgundy slacks and matching sweater. Then with a kiss for Erin, Tara went to meet her husband at the front of the house. In a shower of birdseed, they ran to the car and took off up the coast for their weeklong honeymoon.

An hour later, Matt parked the car in front of the Mill Rose Bed and Breakfast Inn, a Victorian house on the coast. Ten minutes later, he carried Tara over the threshold to their spacious room.

"Oh, Matt. This is beautiful." She glanced around. A huge canopy bed adorned with an ivory comforter was against one wall. A love seat and a pedestal table made a cozy sitting area next to a fireplace.

He set her down. "Not as beautiful as my wife."

She smiled. "I like you calling me that."

"Well, you better get used to it, Mrs. Landers." Matt released her as the bellman brought in the luggage. After Matt handed him a tip, the young man thanked him, then left.

Matt was grinning like a kid, but he didn't care. He'd never felt like this before. His heart rate went crazy as he watched Tara wander around the room, her joy obvious.

"Oh, Matt, everything is perfect. I love it."

"I just want our honeymoon to be unforgettable."

She tossed him a sassy look. "Oh, I have no doubt it will be."

Unable to stay away from her, he crossed the room and pulled her into his arms. "I want you to know how much I love you."

Her arms went around his neck. "Then show me, Matt."

"I plan to," he said, right before his mouth closed over hers. His eagerness was catching, as she melted against him and parted her lips. He moved his tongue inside, tasting, teasing her until she whimpered in need.

He pulled back. "Damn, I want you. Sneaking around for a few stolen moments here and there wasn't enough. But first I want to give you something." He went to his suitcase and pulled out a long velvet box. "This is for you."

"You didn't have to get me anything, Matt. The wedding and honeymoon…"

His quick kiss stopped her protest. "Just open it, Tara."

Tara gasped as she raised the lid and exposed the emerald necklace and matching earrings they'd seen at the Jewel Box. "Oh, Matt, you shouldn't have. They were so expensive."

"You deserve the best, Tara. And I wanted to give you something to remember this day."

She kissed him. "I love you so much. They're beautiful." Her fingers caressed the pendant.

He removed the necklace from the box and slipped it around her neck. He bent and placed a kiss against her skin. "I've had this ongoing fantasy, Mrs. Landers, that on our wedding night, you'll be wearing these emeralds and nothing else when I make love to you."

He turned her around and found her mouth as his hot hands traveled up and down her body. Heat spread wherever he touched her until finally he couldn't wait any longer. He dimmed the lights, then came back to her and began to remove her sweater and slacks. She did the same with his shirt and trousers. Quickly they were both naked and anxious. He stripped back the covers and lay her down, then followed. He looked in her eyes and knew he'd found love. When he entered her body he knew he'd found paradise.

Tara heard Matt cry out her name just as she gasped his, then stars floated around in her head as she let the feeling carry her away. Matt moved next to her, pulling her into his embrace.

She smiled. "I love you."

"I love you," he echoed.

She raised her head. "Was the fantasy everything you dreamed of?"

"And more."

Her hand moved across his chest. "I think I have something else that might top it."

He grinned. "I thought you'd just given me your gift."

"Then I have another." She got up, picked up her purse and brought it to the bed. She sat next to Matt. "Remember the stomach flu I had last week when you made me go to the doctor?"

He looked worried as he nodded. "Why? Is there something you didn't tell me?"

"Sort of. But it's nothing to worry about," she rushed on, feeling her pulse racing with excitement. She took another breath. "As you know, Cari took me to Dr. Kruse, her doctor."

"She's a good doctor," Matt agreed. "Hey, wait a minute, she's an ob-gyn."

Tara drew another breath. "Yes, she said the nausea should pass in a few weeks."

"A few weeks?"

"It seems I'm pregnant." With a shaky hand she pulled the grainy ultrasound photo from her purse.

Matt lay stock-still for what seemed like an eternity, then he jerked up in bed as he accepted the picture. "There has to be a mistake."

Tara shook her head. "Not according to Dr. Kruse. And that picture is our...baby. I told her about your case of mumps, and she only smiled, saying she's heard that story so many times. Dr. Kruse said you had some determined little guppies who did a heck of a lot of swimming to make it to one of my eggs." Tara tried to read her husband's reaction, but couldn't. Tears welled in her eyes. "Oh, Matt, tell me you're happy about this."

He looked up from the picture. "Happy? Tara, happy doesn't describe how I feel. I'm ecstatic. All this time I thought I couldn't have a child." He drew her in his arms. "Oh, God. I love you and our baby so much. How far along are you?"

"Three months. It must have happened the first time we made love. The night of the charity ball."

His brown eyes shimmered with tears. Then he reached over and touched her stomach so reverently she began to well up, too.

"A baby... How do you feel?" he asked.

"Fine." She drew a breath. "Wonderful. I mean I only got the news yesterday...." Her eyes met his. "A baby, Matt. We're going to have a baby—"

He pulled her on top of him and cupped her face in his hands as he kissed her so sweetly she couldn't stop the tears of joy.

"If this is a dream, don't wake me up," he whispered, with awe in his husky voice. "Oh, Tara, I can't believe you came into my life...." He stopped as his fingers caressed her bottom lip. "I'm so blessed to have you and Erin...now you've given me such a gift. A miracle."

"It's a miracle for both of us." Tara leaned down and kissed her husband, knowing that they both had the family they'd been searching for. Her thoughts went to Bri. She was sure that even her sister would be happy about how things turned out.

Tara had found the right Matt Landers.

\* \* \* \* \*

If you enjoyed what you just read,
then we've got an offer you can't resist!

# Take 2 bestselling
# love stories FREE!
# Plus get a FREE surprise gift!

Coming Soon
Silhouette Books presents

*Weddings*
*in White*

(on sale September 2000)

A 3-in-1 keepsake collection
by international bestselling author

# DIANA PALMER

Three heart-stoppingly handsome bachelors are paired
up with three innocent beauties who long to marry the
men of their dreams. This dazzling collection showcases
the enchanting characters and searing passion that
has made Diana Palmer a legendary talent
in the romance industry.

*Unlikely Lover:*
Can a feisty secretary and a gruff oilman fight
the true course of love?

*The Princess Bride:*
For better, for worse, starry-eyed Tiffany Blair captivated
Kingman Marshall's iron-clad heart....

*Callaghan's Bride:*
Callaghan Hart swore marriage was for fools—until
Tess Brady branded him with her sweetly seductive kisses!

*Available at your favorite retail outlet.*

*Silhouette*®

*Where love comes alive*™

Silhouette®

SPECIAL EDITION®

# COMING NEXT MONTH

### #1339  WHEN BABY WAS BORN—Jodi O'Donnell
*That's My Baby!*

Sara was about to give birth—and couldn't remember anything except her name! But a twist of fate brought Cade McGivern to her in her moment of need, and she couldn't imagine letting this unforgettable cowboy go. Still, until she remembered everything, Sara and Cade's future was as uncertain as her past....

### #1340  IN SEARCH OF DREAMS—Ginna Gray
*A Family Bond*

On a quest to find his long-lost brother, reporter J. T. Conway lost his heart to headstrong Kate Mahoney. But with her scandalous past, Kate wasn't welcoming newcomers. Could J.T. help Kate heal—and convince her his love was for real?

### #1341  WHEN LOVE WALKS IN—Suzanne Carey

After seventeen years, Danny Finn came back, and Cate Anderson ached for the passion they'd shared as teenage sweethearts. But Danny never knew that Cate's teenage son was actually her child. Cate hadn't wanted to hurt Danny and her son with the truth. But now she and Danny were falling in love all over again....

### #1342  BECAUSE OF THE TWINS...—Carole Halston

Graham Knight was surprised to learn that he was the father of twins! Luckily, pretty Holly Beaumont lent a hand with the rambunctious tots. But Graham was wary of the emotions Holly stirred within him. For he'd learned the hard way that he couldn't trust his instincts about women. Or could he...?

### #1343  TEXAS ROYALTY—Jean Brashear

Private investigator Devlin Marlowe's case led him to Lacey DeMille, the Texas society girl this former rebel fell for and was betrayed by as a teenager. Now he had the opportunity for the perfect revenge. But he never counted on rekindling his desire for the only woman who had ever mattered.

### #1344  LOST-AND-FOUND GROOM—Patricia McLinn
*A Place Called Home*

When Daniel Delligatti found Kendra Jenner and insisted on being a part of his son's life, Kendra was not pleased. After all, Daniel was a risk-taker and Kendra played by the rules. Could these opposites find common ground...and surrender to their irresistible attraction?

CMN0700